Nine Squares

A TENNIS THEORY, A RETIRED COACH,
A YOUNG GIRL WITH A DREAM

Bruce Reffler

Nine Squares

© 2021, Bruce Reffler.

Paperback ISBN: 978-1-09836-377-2
eBook ISBN: 978-1-09836-378-9

The story you about to read is going to come around uniquely, from the heart of courage, discipline, and persistence, and sprinkled with a goal – the key ingredients to making dreams a reality. As readers of this book, you will learn the secret of life; it's a law that we must obey. God has given all of us unique talents and abilities. Seek, and you will find. God bless, let's begin.

CHAPTER 1

In twenty-four hours, I will be living the last years of my life in a neighborhood that I'm not familiar with, although I've lived there for over forty years. For years I was on autopilot driving to school in the morning. I didn't care about outside circumstances. I was watching the world through a tennis racket.

Austin was wide awake, lying in bed thinking: *what am I going to do with the rest of my life?* A red light was penetrating his pupils. His brain said six o'clock Friday morning. Taking his eyes off the digital clock, he mumbled, "Not even the birds are up, still dark outside." The weather forecast a hundred per cent chance of snow.

Today is the last day I have to get up early for work, thinks Austin. *Who am I kidding? Habits are hard to break. Six o'clock coffee is always a great morning.* Looking across a wave of blankets was Austin's wife, Savanna, snoring like a lion. *With 45 years of marriage, she still thinks she doesn't snore.*

"Where are my slippers?" said Austin, looking at the floor beside his bed. He saw Tarcin, their Cocker Spaniel; he seems innocent with those puppy dog eyes. In reality, he's a slipper thief disguised as a dog. "Do you know where my slippers are, Mr Tarchin?" Austin smiles. "If you could talk, you wouldn't tell me."

Austin walked into the kitchen; morning coffee was always his morning treat. His energy efficiency tied into how many cups of coffee he drinks. Pouring a cup of wake-up was the highlight of his morning. The light was starting to illuminate under the curtains; daybreak prevailed. Sitting at the table with his coffee, Austin was staring at the china cabinet; most homes have dishes and plates and silverware; his cabinet was full of trophies. As a young man, his dreams of becoming a tennis pro were bright; he fell in love with tennis with his father and tennis was his life from that point on. It was ten to seven at the grandfather clock; Austin had to be at the school by eight-fifteen. Hearing the shower, he knew Savanna was up. She was always first in the shower, stealing all the hot water, plus the benefit of Austin, who showered next, would wipe down the glass.

Savanna met Austin at the supermarket at the age of seventeen, her first job. Her first encounter with Austin didn't go well; it was like mixing oil and water. Direct and straightforward, Austin was a know-it-all.

Austin saw Savanna half-naked walking back into the bedroom. "Hey sexy, how's my favorite girl doing today?"

"She's fine; now you better get a move on, its seven-fifteen."

"Do I have to go to school today?" said Austin.

Savanna laughed out loud. "It's not your first day of school, it's your last, and yes, you have to go to school to empty your desk! Tomorrow you can stay home," announced Savanna. "It would help if you hurried; I'm driving you to school today. Do you remember we have to drop my car off to get serviced? You don't want to be late for school on your last day, do you?"

Outside was a winter wonderland, twenty degrees outside with a wind chill of five below. For some strange reason, it felt colder than any other time in Austin's history. Is this the cold feeling of retirement, thought Austin. Austin walked towards the car; the windshield was frozen solid, similar to an ice skating rink without players. After firing up all six cylinders, Austin turned on the defroster then headed back inside the house until the car warmed up.

CHAPTER 2

After dropping Austin's car off at the mechanic shop, they began the short journey across town toward Grand Island High School. "What a beautiful winter day in Nebraska," said Savanna. Looking toward Austin, Savanna said, "You look so sad; what's wrong?"

"I've taught tennis for forty years." Sadness melted into his eyes, his teardrops stopped by his manhood. "I'll miss the interaction."

"Why don't you volunteer at the sports complex? Maybe you'll find your nine squares," said Savanna.

Looking at Savanna, he softly said, "Nine squares, just a dream, couldn't find a girl with that kind of grit, and it probably wouldn't have worked anyway."

"I've seen you with some of your tennis girls. If you stop yelling at them, maybe they won't quit."

"They quit because they don't have grit," said Austin.

"Perhaps you're the problem, and not the girls," said Savanna.

Austin remained quiet as they drove to school. Savanna faced Austin, pulling up to the school. Speaking with her beautiful voice, Savanna said, "It's time to go to school." Austin's brain was rewinding to the first day he stepped on campus as the new P.E. teacher and tennis coach. Time flew faster than a rocket heading to the moon; he wasn't that young kid in the mirror anymore. Savanna broke his train of thought. "You're going to be late. I will pick you up around three."

Austin smiled at his wife and kissed her with sadness in his soul. He said, "See you at three. Love you."

His sadness disappeared as the students yelled out, "Have a good retirement, coach!" Standing still in the moment, he realized just how blessed he's been.

Walking into his office, Austin turned on the lights. The room had a cold, chilly feeling. Clicking on the thermostat and setting the temperature on eighty, Austin said, "That should warm the blood." Sitting at his desk, Austin looked around the room. Books covered every part of his office; it was his book depot. Miles entered the room.

"Good morning," said Miles. Miles was Austin's replacement; Miles has been the assistant coach for nearly five years, well qualified. "Today is your big day," said Miles. "Are you excited?" For the first time in Austin's life, he was speechless to what he heard, as those were the exact words he used on the man he had replaced forty years earlier.

"I'm leaving you all my coaching books," said Austin. "I have read every book in this room; I have no use for them."

"Not even your tennis books?" said Miles.

"You are the new owner."

Miles looked surprised; he also had a concerning heart. "No more tennis?"

"Take a relaxing day; I'll handle things around here today," said Miles.

Austin thought out loud, "I have five school bells remaining on my career." Noticing the picture frame hanging on the door's backside, Austin stood up, grabbed the picture frame off the door, eyed it for a minute, then shoved it into his briefcase. There was no picture inside the frame; inside the structure were nine squares outlined in red, with a caption that said: Nine Squares.

Hearing the fifth bell ring, Austin snatched his briefcase and headed towards the front of the school to wait for his ride. His goodbye tour was over. While he was waiting for his ride; one of his students, Grace, walked up and handed him a present. "What do we have here?" said Austin.

"Open it," said Grace. After removing the Christmas wrapping paper, the gift was a can of new tennis balls. Austin was puzzled. Grace said, "Open the can." Pulling the lid off and unraveling the mystery, Austin dumped one of the three tennis balls into his left hand. Autographs were on all three balls. "All the girls on the tennis team signed the balls," said Grace.

"That was very thoughtful, thank you," said Austin. After receiving a big hug from Grace, Austin's eyes flooded with teardrops. Interrupted by the sound of a horn blowing, his thoughts snapped back into reality; Savanna was here.

Savanna cheered, "You're retired, why the long face? Do you have something in your hand?"

"Tennis balls," replied Austin. "It was a gift from the girls on the team. The girls autographed all three tennis balls."

"That was sweet of them," said Savanna. "I think we can find a spot in our trophy china cabinet."

"Are we going a different way home?"

"Yes," said Savanna. "I have to stop by Alicia's house to drop off the cookies; she lives by Butter Park. It will only take a few minutes." Pulling up to the curb, Savanna said, "Don't go anywhere, I'll be right back."

Austin's eyes zeroed in on the tennis courts on the north side of the park. Not believing his own eyes, there was a girl playing tennis at the park. He grabbed his glasses to reinstate his vision. Austin mumbled to himself, "She's playing tennis in the snow, on a court with no net and no lines." He noticed her tennis racket, it was pink. His mind was interrupted when Savanna opened the car door. As Savanna reentered the car, Austin wanted a second opinion. "Do you see anyone playing tennis over there in the park?"

Squinting to see better, Savanna said, "I don't see anyone, why do you ask?"

Austin intensely stared into the park with his face moving north and south. "Minutes ago, there was a girl on the tennis court playing tennis."

"In this weather?" said Savanna."Your eyes are playing tricks on you. I don't see anyone."

"There was a girl playing tennis in the park, with a pink tennis racket," said Austin.

"If there was, she's gone. Can we go home now?"

Austin nodded his head as to say yes. Pulling away from the curb, they started to head home. "Did Alicia like the cookies?" asked Austin.

Savanna smiled, then said, "Do you want a cookie?"

Austin grinned with a kid-like smile as to say yes.

CHAPTER 3

Two months had passed, springtime was among us. Flowers were starting to bloom, birds mating, and green fields spanned the horizon. The sun arose with all its glory, it was seven o'clock in the morning, Austin's new wake-up time. After coffee, he took Tarcin for a walk to Butter Park. Walking on the right side of the street with Tarcin was no easy task. Being a boy, he had to pee on everything. It had been two months of sitting at the park every day, hoping to see the girl with the pink tennis racket. So far, the only one that was happy was Tarcin; he enjoyed his morning walk. Austin wondered if he'd ever see the girl from two months ago. *Who was that girl on the court*? thinks Austin. His faith in finding her was slowly disappearing.

Entering the house from the front door, Austin removed Tarcin's leash. Most dogs drink after a long walk, not Tarcin. He rubbed his face on the rug, then galloped for his toys. He was a toy fanatic – toys come first, water comes second. "Good morning," said Savanna. "How was your walk? Any luck on finding your tennis girl?"

"No chance. Maybe I saw things."

"I think you should get some city air," said Savanna. "I'm going downtown to do a little shopping; I could use a companion."

Austin laughed. "Let me check my calendar; I had a cancellation. I'm free today. You can treat me to lunch; there's a new restaurant in town called Everything's Good."

Savanna grabbed her sweater and keys and said, "Let's go."

After walking for what seemed like miles, Austin said, "My feet are killing me. Is it time for lunch yet?"

Savanna laid into him with frustration. "You're kidding me, we've only been in two stores."

"It feels like a million," said Austin.

"One more store," said Savanna, "And then I promise you can feed me."

Austin's expression told Savanna he was sorry and also to hurry up.

Austin was sitting on the seat outside the dressing room, waiting for Savanna. Austin always felt uncomfortable in the lady's department. He was looking to the right at the racks of bloomers. And on the left were two racks of bras. Austin couldn't wait to get outside. Savanna walked out from the dressing room with clothes in hand. She said, "Let's head for the register." Austin followed.

Driving into the Everything's Good parking lot was like a traffic jam at a concert; the place was full. "There's a car pulling out of its space upfront," said Austin. Savanna's driving skills were precise; she pulled into the parking spot with ease.

The diner looked old fashion with pictures on the walls with people sitting at tables eating different meals. Chicken, ribs, fish, hamburgers, steak. It had the atmosphere of a home. Entering the café, they was a huge sign that read, seat yourself, please. Austin grabbed Savanna by the hand as they walked towards the open table. "I'm hungry," said Austin. Savanna smiled. After sitting down, Savanna complemented the café, then stretched out her arms to grab Austin's hands.

"Love you!" said Savanna. Austin looked up; their waitress was moments away from impact.

"Good afternoon, I'll be your waitress, here are two glasses of water, my name is Catalina, but you can call me Cat."

"Cat! can we get two cups of coffee, please, before we order."

"I'll be back as fast as a cat," laughed Catalina.

"Her face looks familiar," said Austin.

"Maybe from school?" said Savanna.

"Maybe, but I don't think so."

Catalina returned with two fresh cups of coffee. "Are you ready to order?" she said.

Austin peered at her and said, "Do I know you? What school do you attend?"

"I'm a sophomore at George Town," said Catalina.

"George Town, their tennis team sucks," mumbled Austin.

Catalina announced she was getting off her shift after taking their food order, and a new waitress was coming on board. "We'll eat lunch." Austin's eyesight was on Catalina. As she prepared to exit the restaurant, he noticed she was wearing a backpack with a pink tennis racket shoved in the rear. Pointing out the pink racket to Savanna, Austin said, "She's the girl at the park!" Austin removed himself from his chair to catch Catalina as she headed outside. "Catalina!" called out Austin. Catalina turned around cautiously but quickly. Austin's voice flowed from his lips. "Let me introduce myself; my name is Austin Jones. Have you ever played tennis at butter park in the snow?"

Catalina's mind was processing; how did he know that? Feeling unsure of how to answer, her caution side took over. "Why do you ask?" said Catalina.

Austin laughed. "Let me explain; I was the tennis coach at Grand Island High School for 35 years, just retired two months ago. My wife and I were across the street from Butter Park the day I retired. There was a girl playing tennis in the snow that looked similar to you, and she had a pink tennis racket."

Catalina smiled back. "I love tennis. I play every chance I get."

"Let me ask you a question," said Austin. "Why in the snow?"

Catalina answered, "Why not?"

Austin's heart began racing while his brian waves were saying: she has grit. Could this be the girl I've been trying to find? "Do you play on the tennis team at George Town?"

"No," responded Catalina. "I tried out for the team. The tennis coach told me to use my talent elsewhere."

"Is coach Taylor still there?"

"Yes," said Catalina.

Austin's inner thoughts said: we beat George Town in tennis every year. Maybe it's the coach? "So, you don't have a coach, and you're not on a team?" Catalina shook her head sideways; her answer was no. Austin said, "Would you like one?"

"I guess so," answered Catalina.

"Do you work at the restaurant tomorrow?"

"I'm off on Sunday," responded Catalina.

"If you want to play a game of tennis. I'll be at Butter Park on Sunday, around 8 am," said Austin.

Catalina said, "Maybe I'll see you there." She started skipping down the street, holding her tennis racket.

Austin thought out loud: "Strange."

Walking into the restaurant, he could see Savanna sitting at the table; her lunch was finished. His plate was full of cold food.

"We need a box to go," said Austin.

"Was that the girl in the park?" asked Savanna.

"It was her alright; she's supposed to meet me tomorrow at the park to play a little tennis."

"Are you going to train her?" said Savanna.

"I think so," answered Austin.

CHAPTER 4

Butter Park was empty Sunday morning. The birds were up searching for their morning breakfast. The winds were blowing five miles an hour from the east; it would be a bright sunny day. Austin arrived at the park around seven forty-five AM, delighting in his warm coffee. He released the trunk button from inside the car to get some gear out. Austin then departed from the driver's seat and slowly made his way towards the automobile's back end. He opened the trunk to reveal a tennis store inside the car. Austin grabbed one of his dozen rackets and a can of balls. Then he checked his cell phone to see the time. It was eight o'clock straight up. *We'll see if she arrives*, thought Austin. A moving object in the distance resembled a skateboarder. The skateboarder was jumping curbs as it was arriving at its destination. Catalina arrived out of breath. She spoke in a soft but confident voice, "Good morning, coach."

"Good morning Catalina, is it ok to call you Cat?"

"Everyone else does," said Catalina. Catalina peered into the trunk of Austin's car. "You must have hundreds of tennis balls in there."

"Every ball in there has your name on it," said Austin. "When we play through hundreds of tennis balls, you'll be ready."

"Ready for what?" asked Catalina.

"Your first tournament, a qualifying tournament for the U.S. Open," answered Austin. "Let's see if you can hit a tennis ball over the net."

Austin stood behind the white backline getting ready to serve. He yelled in her direction, "All I want you to do is hit the ball over the net, anywhere you want, do you understand?" Catalina nodded her head in agreement with Austin's demand. Austin served the ball and watched with amazement as Catalina hit a home run deep in center field, landing on a different tennis court. She smiles.

"You said anywhere."

Austin started laughing out loud, causing Catalina to laugh. "That's what I get for saying anywhere," said Austin. "We want to keep it in the lines, on this court, on the ground. Do we understand?"

"Yes," nodded Catalina.

Austin served a definite hit with a speed of seventy-five mph; Catalina quickly neutralized the pace with a winning return on the line. Catalina yelled out from the other side of the green court, "Hey coach, I think that's called my point," she grinned.

"First time luck, that's all that was," said Austin.

He put a spin on his second serve by slicing the ball towards her backhand. Again, she quickly reacted with another winning return on the line. Catalina yelled out, "30 / love!"

Austin thought, *She didn't make the team. The third serve, you either lock on the kill or you go home.* Austin repositioned himself in the center, at the rear of the court. Throwing the ball super high was always Austin's secret weapon for serving. Placement of the ball is always an advantage when you are looking down at an opponent. Giving everything the older man could muster up, Austin's serve blew past the sophomore in high school. It took Austin minutes to stop laughing. "You just got aced by an older man," said Austin. "Come over here. I want to talk to you."

⋮⋮⋮

Cat sat on the bench next to Austin. "How old are you?" asked Austin.

"I'm fifteen and a half."

"You're young to be a waitress."

"My uncle owns the restaurant. I help him out on Saturday."

Austin paused for a few seconds. "I'm here for two reasons. First, I believe in you. I don't know why, but I do. The second reason," said Austin, "Is to see if a theory works. If it does, the only person who will stop you is you. I mean that the training will be so intense you will probably want to quit. I will push you to the breaking point. If you break, it's all over; there's no quitting. If you want out, now's the time. I'm not putting in the last few years I have left with someone that quits."

Catalina clapped her hands. "Did you write that shit?" She laughed. "I'll tell you what, coach, I won't give up on you if you don't give up on me."

They were in sync. "Ok, what time are you finished with school?"

Catalina smiled with enthusiasm. "2:30."

"I'll meet you here at 3 o'clock every day."

"Sounds good," responded Catalina.

Catalina grabbed her skateboard, then said to Austin, "The U.S. Open has the best players in the world. I've never even played in a tournament."

"There are qualifying tournaments before the U.S. Open. If we make it that far, I'm hoping you will get picked for a wild card. I want you to know theirs no guarantee," said Austin.

CHAPTER 5

After seeing his house from a distance, Austin focused on the sidewalk as Savanna was walking Tarcin. Slowing down for a closer look, he yelled out, "Need a lift?"

"I think we can make it from here," laughed Savanna. "How did your new student do today?"

Austin had a puzzled look on his unshaven cheeks. If you were reading his lips, the words would say interesting, very interesting. "I'll meet you at the house," said Austin. "After dinner, well talk about interesting. See you at home, love you."

Austin was sitting in their living room having ice cream.

"So, tell me about interesting?" said Savanna.

"She showed up on a skateboard, jumping curbs, and get this, sliding on a handrail with a skateboard. Then, she aces me twice, hits a home run, and is a total smart ass."

Savanna said, "It sounds like you've found your girl. What's next?"

"We have to get those legs in shape, she needs to be fast and robust. We train every day at 3:00 PM until it gets dark, six days a week. We don't play on Sunday; that's God's day, then we rest."

"Resting reminded me of the recliner. A good book has my name on it," said Savanna. And off she went.

Austin grabbed some of his old books on playing tennis from his office and headed for his recliner. After sitting, he blew the dust off the notepad that he'd had for forty years. The note pad spelled out two words nine squares. Opening the book wasn't easy. Forty years of memories, most of them sad. Flipping through the first page was extremely hard. Time and time again, the pages have failed to produce a prodigy. Austin began scanning the pages with some delight. His dreamed on a theory that was starting to unfold beneath the blankets of reality. After staring and flipping the pages for more than an hour, Austin glanced on the wall; he hung the frame from his office on the wall that said nine squares. *Is it ready?*

CHAPTER 6

Three o clock Monday afternoon, Austin was on the outside of the tennis court, sitting on the bench with his iPad. He was watching drag racing—his second favorite sport. His eyes glanced over his iPad. Catalina was creating havoc on her skateboard, heading in his direction, jumping anything she can find.

"Good afternoon coach," said Catalina. Full of excitement from head to toe, Cat yelled out, "Let's play tennis!"

"First things first," said Austin. "We need to get those legs in shape." Looking towards the skateboard, Austin had an idea. "I want you to skateboard around the outside of the court until I tell you to stop."

Catalina spoke out intensely, "What in the world has that have to do with tennis?"

"Not only will the skateboard help develop balance, but it will also strengthen your legs; if you're going to question my training method, maybe we should go home."

Catalina stared down at Austin as if he was a space alien. "Let's begin," voiced Catalina.

Catalina put down her backpack, then proceeded on her skateboard around the tennis court. Austin continued fiddling with his iPad sitting on the bench; he looked up towards his student every thirty seconds. Catalina yelled out, "Piece of cake, I can do this all day," as she skated close to his feet. He realized Catalina had been skating for nearly twenty-two minutes. Holding his hand out to form a stop sign, Catalina quickly entered the pit area.

"Please turn around and go the opposite way, using your other foot as a paddle." Austin wanted to see if she had balance; most people can't balance using their other foot when pushing a skateboard. Catalina pushed off twice with her other foot before losing her balance and crashing to the ground. "I see we have our work cut out for us," laughed Austin. Cat got up, mad, and jumped back on the skateboard for a second try. This episode only lasted ten feet, down again. Austin couldn't stop chuckling. "OK, we'll have to work on that tomorrow, come over here," said Austin. "I'm going to fill you in on the plan. Years ago, I developed a so-called system for playing tennis using nine squares on each side of the court; when a player on the other side is in one of the nine squares, there's always a square they cannot get the ball. On the other hand, you have to figure out the square you're in and hit it to the square your opponent isn't in, so the other player can't get to it. It's that simple," smiled Austin.

"You need to maintain your mind to control your body," said Catalina.

Austin had never thought of it that way; Catalina was correct.

"There are five things we need to work on," said Austin. "1st serving, 2nd, receiving a serve, 3rd returning the ball, 4th speed, you need leg speed—5th memorization of nine square. You need to know it back and foreword with every possible combination. You have homework not only on the court but off the court," said Austin. "The U.S. Open is six months away. I'm all in if you are."

Catalina grabbed her skateboard and hopped on using her unbalanced leg, and defeated the square. Jumping off her skateboard and thrusting forward with excitement, her hands were in the high five position. Her face and body were dancing on the same floor. "You bet your old ass I'm in." Getting on her skateboard, she headed north. "See you tomorrow, I have to go home. It's my mom's birthday."

Austin watched as Catalina vanished from the park. He mumbled, "Let's go home."

CHAPTER 7

3:00 PM on a Tuesday, Austin was filling his tennis ball machine with 50 balls. *We're going to see how many balls she can get inside the lines. She needs to be in the top five per cent bracket when we head towards the U.S. Open.* Catalina was waiting patiently across the net, waiting on the steel machine to throw the first ball.

"Fire in the hole," said Austin, as ball number one quickly exited the long tube. One by one, Austin used his hand clicker to record the returns. *Let see if she can get past fifty serves*, he thought.

She was starting to miss a lot. "Someone is getting tired." Catalina ignored Austin and continued to pound away. When she finished, he stopped his clicking. Her percentage of inbound shots was only twenty percent. Austin called Catalina over. "Sit down. How does your arm feel?"

"Like jello," said Catalina.

"You made 10 per cent out of a fifty; we have to be at 95 per cent. Tomorrow will work on serving; it's getting late to go home. Just some advice," spoke out Austin. "The more difficult you make it on your opponent, the more times you win."

Catalina wasn't sure she understood, but she was going to find out.

The next day Austin was driving; he noticed someone fooling around inside the tennis court. Giving his pupils time to focus, he realized it was

Catalina. She was skateboarding around the court. Austin was surprised when pulling up to the court; Catalina listened to her music with her headsets on top of her head; she had no clue he was watching. Catalina spun around and headed counterclockwise. She was still having trouble using her right foot. She was wobbling, similar to a tightrope walker. 1, 2, 3, she's down again! Austin was standing on the side of the tennis court, watching Catalina. She kept falling and getting back up, over and over again. Her vision penetrated his vision. Without a word, he know that she was saying: I'm not quitting. Austin returned to the S.U.V. to fetch a bucket of balls. Walking into the court, Austin could see Catalina sitting on the steel bench. "Are you ready to serve, or do you want to go home," smiled Austin. Cat grabbed the bucket and walked to the other side of the court. After serving fifty balls, "Go pick them up," grinned Austin.

The coach pulled his computer out of his briefcase. "What's up with that iPad?" yelled Cat.

He turned with information to her question. "This iPad is our tennis Bible; I keep track of everything we do here; it's my secretary. Now can you please serve." He watched Cat hit the ball into the net fifty per cent or greater, not good numbers for tennis. Austin interrupted Cat. "You need more height on the ball. The goal is to throw the yellow ball three feet over your head; they call it reaching for the moon. It will help if you hit it at the top of your peak. You want to come down on the ball so that you can add power and control. Try it again."

Catalina jumped for the moon and delivered a beautiful shot from heaven. Her face sparkled with pleasure. Catalina was floating on air as she continued to serve. As the afternoon moved on to dusk, Austin measured her success; he moved her up from one to two on the tennis scale.

Sitting next to Cat, Austin knew nothing about his prodigy. "Do you have a family?" asked Austin. "I don't even know your last name."

At that moment in time, Catalina knew somebody would open her life. "It's Davis," said Catalina.

Austin reached out, "Pleased to meet you, Catilina Davis."

"I live on East Dorado in a two-bedroom house with four brothers and two sisters, my mom has two jobs, or we'd be homeless. Any more family questions?" asked Catalina.

"I think that's it," said Austin.

Catalina teared up. "When I win, I'm going to buy my mom a house of her own and give her my winnings so she can retire."

Austin and Catalina wiped away their watery eyes.

"Congratulations, you made it through your first week. Next week on the skateboard, the goal is a hundred times around the court, fifty in each direction; you'll get there in time. Then you will serve fifty balls and receive the same fifty. The fourth thing you have to learn is nine squares. Remember, nine squares can't work without the first three. Get some rest; I'll see you on Monday."

CHAPTER 8

Sunday was a beautiful day; the sun rays were the heat for half the world. Austin and Savanna were on the way home from church; Butter Park was on the right side. Savanna said, "Is that your tennis girl out there skateboarding around the court?"

Austin's attention accelerated off of driving. "I think it is; we don't practice on Sundays."

"She does," said Savanna.

Austin's body kept driving; his mind was thinking: *grit*.

~

Reclining in his car recliner, waiting for Catalina to show up, Austin wondered how one month had flown by since taking on his new prodigy. She had now moved from two to three on the tennis scale. Every day she got stronger and improved. Austin never told her he knew about Sunday.

"The U.S. Open is five months away," mumbled. Catalina would have to up her game, or they wouldn't make it in the first round. You don't have one opponent; you have 300. Catalina skated past the S.U.V. towards the tennis court.

"Good morning," said Catalina. "What's the plan today?"

"Was I thinking? We have five months to train your mind on nine squares. We're going to need help; I have a former tennis student named Grace, shell be free on the first of next month. We need a live person to play against; she

23

will be your only opponent before your first tournament," said Austin. "Are you ready to give fifty laps on the skateboard? Do one set at a time, take your time; I have all day."

Austin settled in for a long afternoon with, of course, his computer. Keeping a close eye on his student, whose legs were beginning to look like jello. Catalina was starting her second set on the skateboard. Austin was laughing and spoke out, "I'm getting tired just from watching." There was only one thing to do; he grabbed an energy drink from his cooler and downed it in 5 gulps; good stuff lingers from his mouth. The next thirty days would fly faster than a rocket. Catalina continued exercising three skills needed to accomplish her dream. Balance, serving, and receiving, her brain has to do the rest.

CHAPTER 9

Sunshine began penetrating the morning sky. It was also piercing Austin's inner eyelids while closed, a red color shining through as sunshine filled the room. It was 6 AM; Austin was sitting on his bed with his hands covering his face, eyes not yet open. Coffee was bouncing around in his head like a gumball machine in motion. Looking at Savanna as she snored away her oxygen, Austin quickly turned his thoughts towards coffee and headed down the hallway toward the kitchen. He grabbed his iPad then headed to the patio.

⁝⁝⁝

"Good morning," said Savanna as she stepped down onto the outside patio, carrying two cups of fresh coffee. "What are you doing?"

"I'm working on nine squares, which entails 81 different combinations to memorize, plus playing tennis."

"Is it even possible?" said Savanna.

Austin looks directly at her and said, "I don't know; it should work in theory."

Savanna threw out some heat: "Let me get this straight, you've been training a girl for two months on a theory that may not work!" The look on Austin's face said" guilty. "You must teach her to win, regardless of nine squares," sounded off Savanna. "Her dreams are in your hands; you need to ask yourself, can she win without it? It would help if you told her the truth; there's no guarantee it will work."

"I already did," said Austin. Knowing that she was right, Austin shook his head in compliance. "She's been ready for a month, physically," said Austin. "Tomorrow is when we'll have Grace. I think it's time for a good old fashioned tennis match."

"Good," said Savanna. "Teach her both ways to play the game; if she falls apart, you'll have back up."

Austin looked at Savanna. "How did you get so wise?"

"I just asked the LORD; he freely gave it to his children."

Austin grinned with breath flowing from his lips, pushing the words out of his mouth, and saying, "Amen."

Austin worked on trying to figure out how to train Catalina on nine squares. Its formula was simple as a chess game, as long as you stayed away from a checkmate. Nine squares is a thief. The other opponent doesn't know he was there until it's too late. Finally, the time was here; nine squares jumped from a dusty old binder into reality—emotions, jump-starts its heart. Austin wanted the door to be open inside his mind. His brain waves were continuously pushing thought.

CHAPTER 10

A car pulled up behind him; glancing at the rearview mirror, he could see Grace sitting in the passenger seat.

"Right on time," said Austin. Meeting Grace by the curb, he said, "Welcome, glad you made it."

Grace looked over at the tennis court. "Is that her?"

"That's her," said Austin.

"What is she doing?" asked Grace.

"She's skateboarding in circles fifty times each way. Then she serves one 50 balls and then returns 50 serves. Then and only then do we start training. When we can't see the sun anymore, we quit," said Austin.

Everything became quiet as four eyes looked at one subject. "If she's that good, you can't run her into the ground," said Grace. "Is she ready for nine?"

"Yes," said Austin. Graces' brain was remembering when she first tried doing nine squares. "When I trained you, we were missing a key ingredient. Visual is what we wear missing," said Austin. "I had you all screwed up; you were thinking on nine squares all the time and not the visual outcome. Grace, you have to give it another try. The U.S. Open starts qualifying in five months. The commitment of all of us is half the battle. You know nine squares better than anyone; we have to fine-tune it," said Austin. Grace smiled with excitement. "It's time to meet Catalina," said Austin.

"Give me a minute. I'll grab my tennis racket," said Grace. After noticing her two coaches on the tennis court's right side, Catalina started to move toward the coach and Grace. Catalina walked up to Grace, intending to get to know her teammate. "Hi, my name is Catalina."

Grace used the handle of her tennis racket to shake her hand. "Hello, I heard a lot of good stuff about you, that you play a mean game of tennis? Is that true?" Grace was testing her honesty; how big is her head, and can it be popped? "Let's mix it up with a little yellow ball and see what we have hiding beneath the sun," said Grace.

Catalina looked over at Austin and nodded her head, and said, "Fair deal."

Austin broke from the pack and walked to his steel bench to watch; this he had to see. Grace was a former junior nationals champion at the age of 12, number 2 in the country. Her mom had been a cancer survivor for nearly two years; Grace took time off to care for her mother. It was time for her to fulfill her dream. Both girls were ready for war; they both have something to prove.

"Let's rally for a little bit to warm up," shouted out Grace.

Catalina stood ready; Grace slammed a mini rocket on the line, right past Catalina.

"We've been practicing," said Catalina.

"Bring it on," yelled back Grace.

Austin's ears popped up, with his eyes focus on them both. Grace slams one into the net. Her second serve rifles toward Catalina, who quickly defeats her opponent, smashing the ball past Grace and hitting the backline with complete accuracy. Catalina's smile was pure pleasure. Grace also smiled and said, "We're all lucky once in a while." Two egos were fighting for respect as the two continued to swap shots back and forth. Austin was speechless; his dreams and vision were in front of his brown eyes.

Austin was giving instructions to the girls. He cut down their skateboard runs to 25 in both directions, receives 25 balls, serves 25 balls, and playing nine squares.

"Three times in a single day. Do we all agree?" said Austin.

Grace questioned Austin in a rejecting tone, "Why do I have to skateboard?"

"We need to build stamina in our legs. If you don't want to skateboard, that's fine. But I need you to run three miles a day." Austin knew Grace hates running.

"I'll do skateboarding," said Grace.

"Are we on the same page?" said Austin. The girls heads wobbled up and down. "Tomorrow all the work begins." In a harsh tone with firmness, Austin said, "In five months, you'll be dreaming nines squares. Get some rest. Grace! Can you give Cat a ride home?"

"Sure, no problem," said Grace.

CHAPTER 11

The next day the two girls were on the tennis court finishing up the 1st three com-mands. Austin was waiting for them to wrap up to launch nine squares. Grace and Catalina finished, then sat down next to Austin for a short break and some water. Austin was holding blue painter's tape in each hand.

"Are we painting something today?" said Catalina.

"We need nine squares on each side of the court," said Austin. "If you have a better way to do this, I am all ears."

Catalina and Grace began taping nine squares on each side of the court with blue painter's tape. After finishing taping, Austin and the girls stared in silence at the squares, wondering if it would work.

"I need Grace to go first; please stand at the net," said Austin. "You have nine squares in front of you; the closest squares to you are the numbers 1, 2, 3, from left to right, the middle 4, 5, 6, and the back 7, 8, 9. I was hoping you could put down your racket and verbally speak and look at the squares 1 through 9 over and over until I say stop. Ready! Go." Austin looked at Cat. "You're next."

"Faster!" yelled out Austin, trying to push Grace to the breaking point. It had been nearly 20 minutes when Austin told Grace her time was up. "Your turn," said Austin, looking at Catalina.

A quiet and indistinct utterance from Catalina was, "This is stupid."

"One though 9, whenever you're ready, let's play dumb," said Austin.

Catalina showed Austin that expression, good come back.

⣿

Catalina stood on number 8 on her side of the net. "Verbally yell out the number and visualize where the squares are," said Austin. "We don't have all day, hurry up!"

Grace and Austin folded their arms and just watched. When Catalina finished her set, her opinion entered her voice box, moved through her lips to sound like she said, "That was too easy!"

"Too comfortable," said coach. "Now please do it backward until I say stop. Go ahead. It will be easy," laughed coach Austin. Grace wasn't laughing, knowing she'd be next. Austin and Grace again folded their arms and just watched. Numbers came to life through Catalina's voice, 9, 8, 7, 6, 5, 4, 3, 2, 1, backward over and over again until her voice was drying up under constant speech. Catalina's breath was similar to snoring, only without the sound.

It was now Grace's turn for reverse numbers. Austin and Catalina folded their arms and just watched. After Grace finished her numbers, Austin was ready to introduce them to phase two.

"You must see them in your mind before your body takes hold." Austin brought Catalina to the center of the court in the front row. "You will throw the ball at one of the nine numbers, whatever number I say, are we ready? I forgot to tell you one small detail; you are going to be blindfolded." Austin reached into his jacket and pulled out a blindfold, handed it to Cat, and said, "Let's begin." Cats' eyes were in a room of darkness, with colors flashing in her eyelids from the sun. "Grace will hand you the balls; when I say the number, you throw the ball at the number and try to keep it in the square." Grace gave her a ball. "With your eyes closed, can you visualize nine squares in front of you?" asked Austin.

Catalina responded, "Yes."

Austin's voice was sitting on top of the wind and heading straight at Catalina. The word seven fell into her ear canals.

"Seven it is." Catalina threw the ball to the back left corner, a dead shot if you aimed a gun at a target. "How did we do?" asked Catalina.

Austin smiled at Grace and said, "Not bad."

Cat and Grace played this crazy game; the girls called it blindfold tennis.

CHAPTER 12

A piece of bread with butter folded in half, with mac and cheese in the middle, Austin's mind was in the past. On the drive home, all Austin could think about was dinner; Savanna's cooking belonged on T.V. The word meatloaf flew from Austin's lips and bounced off the front windshield, into his ears; meatloaf sounds good, hoping Savanna had made meatloaf. Austin saw Savanna in the kitchen, handling food with intense labor. "I hope it's meatloaf," laughs Austin. "What's for dinner, honey?"

Savanna quickly responded, "It's your favorite. Homemade mac and cheese."

"If you are going to eat Mac and Cheese, you have to make a Mac and Cheese sandwich. The sandwich was the best part of the meal."

⁝⁝⁝

Quietly sitting at the kitchen table after dinner, Austin and Savanna were having evening coffee. They would rewind the day and talk out any issues before bed.

"How are the girls doing?" asked Savanna.

"They're doing great," said Austin. "Tomorrow we start phase 3 of training. Their reaction times are faster by the day, and with four months remaining, they will be a force to be reckoned with. My main concern is with Grace; she passed phase 1 but could not deliver on stage 2. She was confused; the check engine light was on in her mind because her brain waves were misfiring," said Austin. "I'm hoping Catalina pushes her over the top with friendly competition."

"Are you sorry you brought Grace into the picture?"

"I have a soft spot for Grace; she was knocking on the door of victory," said Austin. "Then life carries you off in a different direction, only to return a wiser human being."

"That was the heart talking," said Savanna.

"Well, see and witness the future," said Austin.

"I'm going to take a hot bath," said Savanna. "If you want to play, you need to shower."

Austin's ears perked up, with his grin draped around his face. "I'll meet you in the room, and it's not even my birthday or Friday," laughed Austin.

Twenty minutes later, Savanna entered the bedroom with the youth of a younger woman.

"He's snoring," laughed Savanna. "He's going to blame me in the morning for this one. Sweat dreams, honey," and she kissed him on the forehead and said good night.

Austin's eyes pop open, his nose smelled bacon; looking to his right, he realized Savanna wasn't in the place that she previously occupied. The smell of bacon pulled him out of bed. He put on his slippers and robe and headed to the kitchen.

"Good morning sleepyhead. I was just about to wake you," said Savanna. "The coffee is ready; help yourself. Your omelet is cooking."

"What's the occasion?" asked Austin.

"Last night you were terrific."

Austin smiled with self-esteem. "For some strange reason, I don't remember."

Savanna quickly got off the subject; she knew he would ponder it for the rest of the day.

CHAPTER 13

Austin was standing next to the car waiting for the girls to arrive. Looking towards the park's north end, he saw his young tennis stars smiling as they approached the vehicle.

"Good morning, coach!" yelled out Grace and Catalina.

"Morning, girls," said Austin. "We have now trained for four months straight, seven days a week, yes! I know about Sundays. I'm proud of you, girls; if you win or lose, to me, you will always be winners. All I ask is you give nine squares your all. Grace, you have the experience you are going in the first tournament."

"There are more tournaments," said Catalina.

"Both of you will be in different games. When one of you is playing, the other one will be the nine squares coach, following your every more." The girls started laughing; Austin looked suspicious. "What's so funny?" ask Austin.

Catalina laughed. "You need to chill out and have a beer," she said. Grace and Catalina burst up with laughter.

Austin smiled. "Thanks for reminding me; we need to laugh." Austin opened his truck, pulls out two brand new tennis rackets, handed them over to the girls, and said, "Let's get out of here."

They were heading down the highway at illegal speeds. It was early Thursday morning, the day before the tournament. Austin and the girls stayed quiet on the drive; nerves were tight, excitement filled the air. He woke the girls from a boring car ride to see that the stadium was upon them. Both windows went down, Catalina and Grace were acting like two dogs looking out the window.

"Open this door and let me go!" screamed Catalina. Grace starts to bark, and Catalina starts to howl. Austin laughed and pushed the button to raise the glass; everyone was laughing.

After checking in at the stadium, the three of them headed for the hotel. Austin said, "Have a good night," in the elevator and watched the girls exit on floor 6. "Get some rest. We have a big day tomorrow."

As soon as Austin fell out of sight, Cat & Grace ran for the elevator, heading for freedom. As they opened up the door right in front of them was Austin. "Where are you going, girls?" asked Austin.

"Nowhere," said Grace.

"That's what I thought," said Austin. "Let me make sure you get to bed because if you sneak out one more time, I'll pull you from the tournament. Do I make myself clear?"

"Yes," said both girls at the same time.

"OK, see you in the morning," said Austin. Austin got off on his floor and headed to bed. The girls also went to bed.

Walking into the arena was exciting for Catalina. Catalina was singing in the car on the way, "Show me the crowd, baby!" She loved crowds.

Catalina yells out as we entered the arena, "There's no crowd here, where is everybody?"

"When you start at the bottom, you have very few spectators," laughed Austin. "The judge will be here in one ½ hour. Cat, warm her up, please." Austin looked out across the net, sitting on a steel bench, watching the two girls warm up brought so many memories. Austin wakes up and yells out, "Nine squares!" with a firm voice. Grace hit square nine. "Good job Grace," said Austin. He yelled out, "5, 2, 7, again! Good job." Grace continued to improve on nine squares. "OK, bring it in!" says Austin.

While the girls were sitting on the bench drinking water, the moment was upon them. "The girl we're facing today is from Long Island; she's won three junior titles. She is an average player; her weakness is her serve; take her out fast and let's go home," said Austin.

Walking into the arena was Grace's challenger; her name was Alicia Taylor, not far behind her was the judge, a relatively small fellow with a tennis cap on his head. She was wearing a pink coat. The stands were filling up with about three dozen people. After going over the rules with both girls, it was now time for tennis. Grace won the coin toss; she would be up first. Grace grabbed her new tennis racket, walked onto the court, and met Alicia in the middle of the net to shake hands.

Warming up had come to an end; the game was about to begin. Grace rifled a fast spinner towards her opponent, catching the outer line, 15/ love. Serving was Grace's favorite. The second serve knew where it was going.

Alicia slammed the ball with intensity towards Grace. Grace runs towards the net like a track star and blocks the ball's approach. 30/love. Grace continued with a command performance, not letting Alicia gain traction. In ten minutes, the first game was over. Austin stood back and watched Grace destroy her opponent 6,2 and 6,3 in straight sets to move up to the second round. Grace came running from the court with her hands quivering in excitement, and hugged Catalina. Austin said, "Grab your stuff, let's go."

As Austin headed for the car, the girls said, "What's his problem?"

Walking away from the arena, Austin said to Grace, "You didn't play nine squares. Why?"

"She was too easy of an opponent; I didn't need nine squares."

Austin smiled, then said, "Good job."

Graces' smile was pure joy. Screaming broke out in the back seat. Catalina was congratulating Grace with a hug.

After dinner, Austin said, "Listen up, girls, grab some me time, and get some rest tomorrow. We have two matches to get through on Saturday. Sunday will be the final, and this place will be wall-to-wall spectators."

Grace was a show-off; the greater the applause, her ego expands, and the coach knows when to fuel the fire.

CHAPTER 14

Getting woken up by a phone call is the worst feeling, unnatural, a noise from hell. Catalina answers the phone and hears another machine telling her to get up. Catalina looks over at Grace with an eye open, her mouth wide open, exposing a bear-like sound. "Grace! Wake up," says Catalina.

"Five more minutes, please."

Austin was waiting in the lobby for the girls to arrive. When the elevator doors opened, the inside light returned to its natural environment. Popping out of the elevator like popcorn cooking in a bag, they spotted the coach. "Quit sitting around, coach; that's all you do," says Catalina. "Let's go; we have a big day."

Austin grins, and his face muscles laughed, then he said, "Let's go."

Arriving at the arena for Grace's second day of competition was causing great enthusiasm and eagerness. Austin's job was to keep the girls grounded; the airspace in their minds is closed. The instructions for today are simple: let see if nine squares works.

Her next opponent was Lisa Woods, a senior from Florida with wealthy parents.

"She's an A-rated player, a tough player who reaches the top but never goes down the winning side; though she reached the finals last year. Don't slip up, or she'll get you," said Austin.

Grace was holding a hot cup of coffee with one hand and a racket with the other. Grace's vision was scouting the crowd. There were more than a hundred spectators; the public was multiplying fast. "Huddle time," yelled out the coach. "On the serve, listen up, let the ball go one-shot normal, and start nine squares on the second shot. Catalina is writing down the numbers you should be hitting on. If we keep track, we can improve accuracy. May nine squares be with you," laughed Austin. "I like that line."

Catalina pulled out the rolling eye routine and said, "Is that what you do when you retire? Watch space movies? Exciting," laughed Catalina.

Austin laughed, then found his seat for the second tournament. Catalina settled in the front with a long net angle. Grace started warming up her muscles; her body's inner strength had to stretch to be flexible.

"We will now begin the match," yelled out the referee. Woods won the coin toss; with that, she could choose which side of the court she wanted and the decision to serve first. Austin glanced over at Catalina and nodded his head; they were ready. Woods served the first ball into the net. That gave Grace the advantage. Grace smacked a hard shot directly towards Woods, who returned it at Grace; she hit it straight at Woods, who returned the shot straight down the right sideline for a point.

"What the hell is she doing?" mumbled the coach. "Her instructions were to start nine squares on the second shot."

Austin's hands spread apart, showing a feeling of disgust. Quickly turning in the direction of Catalina, Catalina responded the same way. Grace continued to do it her way; it cost her the first set. 6-4. On the break, Austin and Catalina sit next to Grace on the steel bench. Grace's feelings were down next to the gutter. The coach's job was not only to train her; he also had to encourage her. Catalina put her arms around Grace and smiled. Catalina said, "You can win this game," with a sweet voice.

The old demons of nine squares are telling her she can't do it, Austin thought.

Austin stared into her eyes. "You have to let it go. If you only achieve half the points from nine, you could win this game."

Grace stood up and said, "Let's win."

"OK," said Austin. "That sounds like a winner. What do we do after the second shot?"

"Nine squares," sounded off Grace.

"Atta girl," said Austin, with an amused expression showing the corners of his mouth turned up. "Times up, get out there and win this match, and let's go home."

Grace's brain was telling her; *he always says that.*

The whistle blew for the second set to start. Grace made her way to the court's backline. Looking towards Austin and Catalina, Grace nodded her head. "Let's begin!" yelled out the referee.

Grace waddled back and forth, anxiously waiting. Woods' first serve hit the net at 87 miles an hour. Throwing her second serve high into the air for efficiency, the ball landed in front of Grace; she returned the yellow ball at Woods, who slammed the ball to the court's opposite side, scoring the first point with a line shot. Woods is leading 15 / love. Grace battled back and forth on the next serve, trying to set nine squares in motion; Woods forced Grace to play her game, Woods scored again. Advances 30 / love. Woods scored two more points, ending the game. Grace's turn to serve. She hit a powerful shot toward Woods, who quickly returned the ball directly in front of Grace. Grace was standing on square 3, Woods on square 7. Austin yelled out, "6!"

Graces memory woke up, but was still confused, hitting square 9 instead. Woods ran it down, returning the shot. Catalina's verbal tongue sounds off,

"4!"; Grace slammed the ball with a grunting noise toward square 4, hitting 4 inches from the line, and scored the point. Austin and Catalina screamed with rejoicing, as the crowd and referee turn around with puzzlement.

"Can we please keep it down?" said the referee.

Austin's inner thoughts were speaking to himself: *nine squares worked*! Grace was ahead 15 / love. Grace threw the yellow ball over her head and stretched her body to its fullness. Woods slammed the ball back at Grace. Austin watched intensely, hoping Grace followed through using nine squares. Grace's eyes focused on square 6 then backhanded the ball, aiming at 6; Woods literally dives for the ball and surprisingly returned it toward Grace's 7, with a soft hit with a seven-degree angle, Grace rushed the net and delivers the ball straight towards 7, and hit the backline and scores. Catalina cheered as the format of nine squares worked again. Grace continues on the path of victory, winning the second game; by mixing nine squares with essential tennis, Grace won six games to four to tie the match. With one more set standing in the way, Austin knew it was a critical moment for Grace. Austin sat down next to Grace on the bench.

"Good job, how do you feel?"

"Good," said Grace.

"OK, we have one more set to go. Use nine squares as much as possible. Don't let Woods get the jump on you."

After switching sides, it was Woods' turn to serve. With a command performance, Woods took the early lead by catapulting three straight line shots. With the score being 40 / love, Austin called for a time out. Catalina and Austin sat next to Grace, whose enthusiasm was negative.

"Just because she serves better than you doesn't mean she can beat you," said Catalina.

Grace laughed. "Thank you for the encouragement."

"That's what I'm here for," laughed Catalina.

Austin asked, "What is going on out there?"

"Woods' backhand is weak after using her forehand," said Catalina. "Keep the pressure on the backhand; 1, 4, 7 using nine squares is your strength. All we need is five straight points," smiled Catalina. Austin's words were silent; Catalina said it all.

The stress on Graces' face looked like a volcano that was about to rupture. Woods served as an act of concentrating, she fired a direct hit in front of Grace, sandwiching her shot, causing the ball to drop inches over the net on square 3. Woods was too far back to react, Grace got the point, though it was a shot from Luckyville U.S.A. Austin eyed Catalina, Catalina eyed Grace, Grace eyed Austin with the expression of: that was to close. The score was now 40 / 15. Grace readied herself for Woods' serve; the yellow ball slammed into the net, giving Grace a more comfortable second shot. Grace hit square 6 with an outside shot to win the point. It was now 40-30. Austin knew Woods wasn't going to make the same mistake twice. He crossed his fingers as Woods served a blessing serve straight at Grace. She steps away from nine squares, hitting right back at Woods, who quickly got on top of the ball and overpowered Grace, causing her to stumble to the point of no return. Woods won the game. Woods tried to capitalize on her win, serving a perfect shot into Grace's racket; Grace struck back with a solid return, trying to set up nine squares with a direct hit towards square 9. Woods backhanded the ball crossing the net, and landing on square 4. Grace stretched her backhand; she hit a line shot straight down the court's west side for the win love/15. Austin's mouth says, good job. He knew Grace had to get past Woods' serve to pull out a victory. After serving, Woods ran to the net to intimidate Grace. Grace's shot fell into the net. 15/15. Woods was noticing a shortcoming in Grace's plan. She attacked the net every shot, shutting down her arduous search for the win.

Nine squares were becoming quiet in their ability to perform; it wasn't nine's fault; circumstances just overpowered it. Grace lost the third set of 6 games to 3. Grace's dreams were on hold; for now, Catalina hopped over the small fence and headed towards Grace, who was in tears, and give her a big hug. At the same time, Catalina peeked over Grace's left shoulder towards where the coach was sitting; Austin was gone. *Where did he go?* thought Catalina.

Grace and Catalina walked over to the metal beach to gather Grace's things. Grace remarked, "Where's the coach?"

"I don't know," said Catalina.

As Grace and Catalina walked through the parking lot, they could see Austin sitting in his car. "Are you OK?" said Catalina.

Austin said, "I'm fine, now let's go?"

The ride home felt like a gloomy rainy day; Austin didn't say one word all the way home.

CHAPTER 15

Savanna was surprised to see Austin; as he entered the house, she knew something was wrong, just looking at his face.

"Do you want to talk about it?" speaks Savanna.

Turning his thoughts in her direction, he said, "Grace lost the second round."

"Sorry to hear that," said Savanna.

"The net beat us," said Austin.

Savanna was confused. "What exactly do you mean?" she asked.

"When Woods rushes the net, Grace's response was causing nine squares to fail almost every time. I'm going to take a shower then head to bed."

The next morning, Austin was sitting at the table drinking his coffee. Savanna walked in.

"Good morning honey,"

"Good morning dear, would you like me to make you breakfast?"

"Please." said Austin.

As Savanna was cooking, she knew the question had to come up. Was Austin done with his nine squares theory? Sitting face to face drinking coffee, Austin could see the look on his wife's face. Austin said, "I was done with tennis when I came home last night; I felt I let Grace down. That hurt me more than anything." Tears ran down his face.

Savanna rose to her feet and hug him from behind. "If you quit now, you not only let yourself down, you let Grace and Catalina down also."

Austin started crying; he knew his wife's words were real. Austin was sad to hear that Grace blamed him for her loss. "She said nine squares cost her the game."

"You've known Grace for a long time," said Savanna. "Time heals broken hearts. God will mend her heart; it's our job to pray for her." Austin agreed. "Can you fix nine squares?" said Savanna.

"I don't know," said Austin.

Eight o'clock Monday morning, Austin was waiting for Catalina at Butter Park. He wanted to hear her opinion on Grace and nine squares. Catalina walked up from behind Austin's car and entered the passenger seat. Eye to eye, Austin said, "What do you want to do?"

"I want to play tennis," said Catalina.

"How do you feel about nine squares?" he asked.

"When I go home, all I think about is studying all the possible combinations for nine; I'm ready."

"OK," said Austin. "Our tournament starts Friday."

"Let's get to work," said Catalina. Austin smiled.

The Friday drive was full of fun; Catalina and Austin sang to the radio to the stadium; Catalina was glad to see Austin loosening up, moving back in forth while singing. Cat's first match was against Taylor Jones, much older, with several tournaments under her belt. Catalina led the path towards the locker room to get ready; Austin made his way to the stands. Jones was already on the court warming up. Austin was observing the young lady, trying to find an imperfection. Catalina appeared from the locker room with a youngster-like feeling. She was smiling from ear to ear, bouncing around in a clueless state. Austin called Catalina over.

"What's up, coach?" said Cat.

"You know what to do, so what are you doing?"

"Playing dumb," answered Cat. Austin has a puzzled look on his face. "If she thinks I don't know what I'm doing, she won't see the beating I'm going to give her."

Austin thought, *In all my years of tennis, I've never met anyone stranger than Catalina.*

Catalina won the coin toss; she would get to severe first. Cat's equilibrium completely changed. She was in kick-ass mode. Cat threw the yellow ball high over her head; it blew past Taylor at more than a hundred miles an hour. Taylor had no chance. Catalina scored 15/ love. Austin said, "Where did that come from?"

Catalina's second serve returned to her backhand. Catalina needed squares 3, 6, or 9 to activate nine squares. Cat popped a soft shot over the net in square 3, the hardest nine shot. Taylor ran for the net, two feet short of reaching the ball; all she could do was watch the ball bounce twice. The score was now 30/ love.

Catalina's third serve dropped in front of Taylor as if it was in slow motion, as if Cat wanted her to hit the ball. Bouncing right in front of her, Taylor returned the serve deep into the backcourt; Cat quickly sprinted towards the ball and returned the ball straight at Taylor; it fell in square 7, Taylor's forehand delivered the ball on Cat's 5 square. Catalina's eyes focused on Taylor; she was still standing on square 7; Cat's priority was to survive; she aimed for square 6, again hitting her mark; the crowd went crazy, cheering for her. Cat nodded to her fans. Austin smiled from his heart, whispering to himself, "Go, girl, go."

The score was now 40/love. Catalina needed one more point; Austin was crossing his fingertips. Catalina stared down Taylor; then, she looked at the coach. She tossed the ball at the exact point as the first severe; she power slammed the yellow ball, blowing it past Taylor for her first game win; the crowd was in awe. Catalina continued with high pressure throughout the first set. Her skateboard legs were tireless. Nine squares exceeded their expectations. Taylor didn't win a single game in the first set. Austin jumped out of his chair with excitement. Catalina headed to the other side as if she's done this a hundred times before. Catalina continued playing like a champion, out powering, outperforming Taylor on every step of the way to victory. She only needed one more game to advance. It was now Jones's turn to serve. Jones hit a stunning hard shot that blasted past Catalina to take the early lead 15/love. Jones wasn't going down without a war. Catalina returned the second serve; the rally was a battle; neither side was losing, as shots fired back in forth—Jones grunted as she hit a line shot to win the point. The score was now 30/ love. Catalina was struggling to set up nine squares. The last thing Austin wanted was a third set between the two players. He signaled Cat to call a time out.

He pointed at her shoes. He needed an excuse to talk to Catalina; she motioned to the referee her tennis shoes are loose and needs to tie them. Austin met her at the steel bench while she pretended to re-tie her shoes.

"It would help if you let nine squares go; we need to win this game," said Austin. "Pressure her backhand."

Catalina smiled and headed back on the court. Jones's third serve hit the net, which gave Cat an advantage. Her second shot hit the top of the net and fumbled in for a point; Jones led 40/love. Cat readied for the serve, wiggling back and forth. Jones hit another net shot. Austin clinched his fist as if to say we needed this big time. Her second shot was much slower; Cat moved in with aggression, slamming the ball towards Jones's backhand and hitting the white line; she scored. It was now 40/15. Another fierce rally as Cat stayed on the attack, Austin watching intensely with right and left head movements. Cat ran towards the net and blocked Jones's projectile and scored, the score was 40/30. Jones double nets; the playing field is deuce, 40/40. Austin crossed his fingers; Jones's interior thoughts were doubting. Jones hit the net on her first serve. Austin's feelings were so tight he felt like he had to unzip his skin. Catalina returned the second ball in Jones's direction. She returned the ball at a low level, hitting the net. Catalina's advantage. Jones's next serve was desperation. She hit a bullet serve with promise, only to miss its mark as Catalina grabbed hold with her racket and sent the yellow ball on the line for the game. Austin raised his fist and extended his arm for victory. Catalina's composure stayed steady while shaking Taylor's hand at the net, then she ran and jumped into Austin's arms with tears of excitement reflecting off her face.

"Well done," said Austin.

After celebrating with lunch, Austin drove Catalina home. On the car ride, Catalina was glowing like a lit Christmas tree.

CHAPTER 16

Austin entered the house and noticed Savanna was in the kitchen making cookies.
Austin grabbed her from behind with a kiss on the neck; chills reached her spine.

He whispered in her ear, "Catalina won."

Turning around, Savanna noticed for the first time in a long time, a sparkle in her man's eyes. The excitement lasted until bedtime as Austin's tongue finally stopped talking. Austin fell asleep, cuddling against his wife. Round two was hours away.

On the second day of the tournament, Cat's opponent was Ronnie Mills, a tall, twenty-two-year-old with long legs. She looks more like a runner than a professional tennis player. Long legs are dangerous; they can usually outrun their opponent. Catalina only had three hours of sleep; she ran nine squares in her mind all night long. Austin wasn't happy; she needed rest. He was pleased with her intellectual drive. Catalina continued to win while in the second round, beating Mills two sets out of three. Catalina won using nine squares. Catalina was in the semi-finals on Sunday morning; the final round would be on Sunday night; two games on the same day was a tough day.

Saturday night was full of hope; Austin and Savanna were talking in the living room about Saturday. Savanna questioned him on Catalina's progress, he responded with almost an impossible dream of every coach. "Some players have a natural ability. Others have to be formidable talent, but very few have the courage and resolve and strength of character in every breath they take. Catalina's inner tank is full."

Savanna smiled, stood up and kissed her lifelong coach and husband, and headed to bed. Savanna would experience the game on Sunday for herself.

The early morning was full of spectators; as Austin and Savanna walked towards the central court, he could hear people talking about Catalina, calling her the supergirl of tennis. Savanna laughed. "Are you the one that's promoting her, not me?" said Austin. "She is doing that all on her own, you'll see." The two older love birds grabbed each other's hands as they made their way into the area. Catalina was all in pink and on the court signing autographs.

"Do you think this is going to her head?" said Savanna.

"I hope so," replied Austin.

Her actions mesmerized Catalina fans. They didn't know whether to applaud her or call bravo. As she made her way over to Austin and Savanna, she spoke out about the plan. Savanna commented on her pink and white earrings. "Pretty, where did you get them?"

"At the ninety-nine-cent store," smiled Catalina.

Savanna's trying to figure out Catalina; her inner thoughts keep saying: no internet connection at this time.

"Your opponent is Ginger Weber, a twenty-one-year-old, a good player, well schooled, and well trained. It's Ginger's third try at the U.S. Open. Her weak spot is long rallies; she gets tired, then starts hitting the net. All you have to do is outlast her; it's that simple."

Hearing the referee yell out game time, Catalina walked to the court's center for the game toss. The silver coin lands on heads, Ginger, would serve first. Savanna's head scanned the attendance; her elbow nudged Austin's arm while her head turned in the crowd's direction. Two young girls were holding up signs that said, "Go, Cat, go." They both smiled with delight.

Catalina walks back in forth in her pink bubble gum dress, Waiting for the serve. Ginger served a 91 mph serve to Catalina's forehand, her tennis racket collided against the yellow ball, pushing it hard to the other side. The power struggle to win on the first serve could put doubt in the opponent's mind. Catalina was running Ginger all over the court. Waiting for an opening on square 6, she finally stepped through and won the point, love/15. Catalina rushed the net on the second serve, dropped the ball in square 1 for an easy point; love/30. Ginger slammed a line shot past Catalina's backhand and scored, 15/30. The play continued as Ginger rushes the net; Catalina ran toward the net as Ginger burned a hard hit into the court's back left corner and scored. 30/30. Ginger served another line shot past Catalina to take the lead 40/30. Ginger released a blistering 95 mph fastball, Catalina hit it into the net. Ginger won the first game as the two players made their way to the bench for water.

Austin approached the bench in a manner of hopefulness. He said, "Do you know the problem?"

Cats' voice was out of breath as she said, "I'm not outlasting her."

"Fix the problem if you want to win." Austin then returned to his seat.

Cat walked on the court to fix the problem. She knew her dreams were on the chopping block. Catalina served with boldness; the fight was on. After a long rally of twelve hits, Cat won the marathon.15/love. Catalina's next serve hit the court, similar to a wave crashing into the shore, dropping it hard in front of Weber as she slammed the ball into the net. 30/ love. After the second return, Catalina smacked the ball in a specified place to receive nine squares to prevent Weber's fair shot. Catalina succeeded, 40/love. Catalina raced to victory with a 105 mph serve that any race car driver would be proud of; Catalina smoked her opponent, tying the match one game apiece. Catalina continued working on the problem by setting up nine squares. Long rallies weren't a factor as long as nine squares were being influential. The battle would last 1 1/2 hours, both players were exhausted, but Cat would win 2 out of 3 sets to win the match.

CHAPTER 17

With the finals six hours away, Catalina's stamina would be pushed beyond her limits.
Sitting on the painted blue lunch table, Savanna was getting to know Catalina as they were eating. Austin disappeared for a while; he was scouting out Catalina's next opponent. After an hour of small talk, Austin reappeared on the scene, carrying two hot dogs with mustard and relish and two side orders of French fries. After kissing Savanna on the cheek, Austin directed his voice straight at Catalina. "How are you holding up?"

"My legs are tired; my feet hurt, my arm is a little sore; other than that, I feel great."

"No pain, no gain," said Austin.

"Who's my next opponent?"

"Her name is Ann Thomas, I don't want to tell you, but you have to know, she demolished her adversary from achieving her goal, she won two straight sets. Here are the keys to the car; take an hour nap to rest your mind and body. The game starts at 6 o'clock, meet us at five, at the grandstands."

Watching Catalina walk away, Savanna asked, "Can she beat her?"

"Not without number nine," said Austin.

"How's she doing with nine?" says Savanna.

"She has the mental part down, but after that last match, the physical part worries me."

It was now 15 minutes past five, and still no sign of Catalina. The grandstands were starting to fill up with spectators. Savanna spotted Catalina entering the outer gate as if she was a spectator. Since this was her first tournament, her face was unfamiliar with the crowd. "Where have you been?" asked Austin.

"Sleeping, that's what you told me to do."

"OK, hurry up and change."

Austin grabbed a new tennis outfit from his brown duffel bag and tossed it in Cat's direction; the outfit was fluorescent green. "I like the colors," said Catalina.

"Good, now take off that bubble gum outfit and put the new one on." Austin was working on her image; sometimes, a picture is everything.

Fifteen minutes later, Catalina jogged into the area, wearing a green glow stick, capturing the crowd's attention. She sat down in front of Austin for coaching. "Are you ready?" said Austin.

"Not really I'm a little sore."

"Ready or not, we need it to win this match. Remember, after the second return starts setting up nine squares," Austin told her with the plain truth, with encouragement, "You remember hitting the ball in the snow?" Catalina nodded her head. "That's how I want you to play this game; you need to feel it, not see it."

Catalina's eyes penetrated deep into Austin's eyes; she then turned around and walked on the court to warm up.

Austin sat next to Savanna, grabbed her right hand; the game was ready to begin. Catalina won the coin toss; she would serve first. Catalina threw the yellow ball four feet over her head; her tennis racket became a powerful weapon, hitting the moving object towards her opponent. Thomas returned the serve straightforward into Catalina's path; she quickly jumped on the return, trying to set up nine squares. Thomas smashed back an almost perfect line shot to take the first point of the game. The score is love/15. Catalina took a hurried look at Austin. He gave her a pushdown look with his hand as to say: stay calm. Powering the second serve with a line shot caught Thomas off guard; the score was now 15/15. On the third serve, Catalina returned the second serve, hitting square 9; Thomas ran it down, smashing it directly in front of Catalina. She backhanded it on square 4 for the point. Nine was doing its job. Catalina was ahead for the first time; the scoreboard read 30/15. On the next serve, Thomas rushed the net. Catalina leaped in front of her, blocking the shot with a sideways hit to square 1, resulting in a 40/15 lead. Before Catalina's next serve, Austin noticed she was rubbing her right arm. The soreness was from the great battle 4 hours ago. Catalina served a hard shot; an anguished sound escaped from her lips as she aced Thomas for the win. Game one is in the history books. Austin said to Savanna, "We will need ice; go down to the locker room and see if you can get us an ice pack."

Austin leaped out of his seat. He reaches Catalina, and then yelled to the referee, "We need a time out. Tell me, how do the arms feel?"

"A little sore."

"On a scale of 1 to 10?" Austin waited for her answer; if she says ten, he would have to pull her from the match.

Catalina's voice sounded out the word four.

"OK," said Austin, "We need the arm to win two straight sets; if not, the arm may not last. What do you think?"

"If I have to play with my left hand, I will; I'm not quitting."

"OK," said Austin, "You need to beat her in two straight sets using nine squares. Now let's go out there and kick her ass."

Catalina slowly walked back on the tennis court, Austin returned to his seat. Savanna reappeared with an ice bag in her right hand. "How is she doing?" asked Savanna.

"Her pain in her arm is at a level 4; if it gets much worse, I'm going to have to pull her. She needs to win both sets to win this match," said Austin.

Savanna said, "And if she doesn't win?"

Austin replied, "Her dreams might become memories."

Thomas's preparation was in full throttle and ready to serve. Catalina played deep, Thomas's first serve hit the top of the net, slowing down the ball; Catalina ran to her own square 8, saw Thomas is still standing on her square 7; Catalina tapped the yellow ball into square 3 and unless Thomas had a pair of wings, she wasn't going to make it in time. The ball rolled off the court; love/15. Thomas fired a strong serve, Catalina's return hit the net. 15/15. Catalina started depending on her backhand to absorb the pain from her right arm. Thomas saw that Catalina was favoring her right arm. Thomas continued serving to Catalina's right side. Cat kept nine squares alive and breathing. Scoring point after point to take the first set, seven games to five.

Sitting on the bench next to Catalina, Austin's first and only question is, "What's your pain level?" Catalina was too scared to speak. "I'll ask you one more time," said Austin. She continued her silence. "I'm going to call the game." Austin knew a temporary injury is better than one that's permanent.

"Seven," said Catalina. With tears running down her eyes, she pleaded with the coach. "It's my life, not yours."

Austin stared her down, then said, "OK, it's all yours," then headed to his seat.

Catalina places the racket in her left hand, stood up then headed to the court.

"She's playing left-handed," said Savanna.

Austin responded, "I didn't know she could play left-handed." Austin had an uncertain look on his face. Thomas started the second set with a bang forcing the ball towards Catalina's left arm as she tried to carry on the operation of nine squares. Thomas was betting on her two out of three serves to win four games in a row. Austin put his head down; he couldn't watch.

Savanna grabbed Austin's attention. "She is starting the fifth game right-handed."

Catalina rubbed her right arm, trying to heat the muscles. Catalina toppled the hundred-mile an hour mark. Thomas struck the ball covered with fibers creating a smooth surface back in Catalina's direction. She has to set up nine squares on the first return to minimize her swings. Hitting square 9 opened up square 4. Catalina's return hit the center of the bullseye for the point, 15/love. Catalina rushed the net on the next serve and blocked the incoming with her racket onto square 2 for the win, 30/love. She got a break when Thomas's ball lost strength then hits the net, 40/love. Austin crossed his fingers using his right hand. Savanna looked on with an uncertain outcome. Catalina aced Thomas and won her first game. Catalina continued one of the strongest comebacks in amateur history, using nine squares to tie the match four games apiece. Catalina's arm felt like a rubber band. After receiving the first point with a net fault. Catalina flung off her shoe on purpose, using the excuse to talk to the coach with a time out. Austin ran towards the bench and pretended to fix her shoe.

"How's the arm?"

"Still moving," says Catalina.

"Good responses," said Austin. "We need seven straight wins to win this game. Your reserve tank has eight wins left with one spare." Austin smiled, and then said, "Visualize it, and let's go home."

He stood up and headed to the grandstands. Austin said to Savanna, "Seven to go."

Thomas's second serve hit just past the outer bounds line, an easy point for Catalina love/30. "Six to go," mumbled Savanna, looking over at Catalina, who continued to rub her right arm. On the third serve, Catalina smashed the ball in her opposite direction; Thomas fired back with a hard hit, Catalina hit it before trying to set up nine, but Thomas continued the back in forth game, not giving Catalina the opportunity for a winning shot. Thomas drove the ball low into the net; Catalina now led love/40. Thomas got nervous as she cut two balls into the net. Catalina not only won the game, but she also won four straight serves. The crowd that was chanting for Thomas changed their tune and cheered for Catalina. Austin calls for a time out. Austin reaches the steel bench first with the ice pack. As soon as Catalina sat down, he draped the ice pack on her right shoulder. "Good job," said Austin. "We had two lucky breaks. How the arm?"

"It hurts," responded Catalina.

"What's your pain now?"

She said, "It's a 9."

"Can we get four more serves out of it?"

"I think so," said Catalina.

Austin looked over toward the Thomas camp; they knew she was hurt. When a player is injured, you go for the kill. "After you serve, use two hands on the racket."

Catalina made her way back on the court and was ready to serve. Savanna crossed her fingers and her toes. Catalina tossed the ball high over her head; she hit the net with a low serve. Her next serve had to slow down to guarantee it would make it over the net. Thomas returned the ball to square 4; Catalina applied a two-handed backhand that forced a volley. Thomas ran for the net like a goalie playing hockey; Catalina popped the ball ten feet over Thomas's head. It landed on square 8; Thomas would have needed a car to reach it; Catalina won the point, 15/love. The silence of the crowd was frightening; you could hear a pin drop. Catalina's serves were slowing down to eighty-one M.P.H., leaving a massive opportunity for Thomas. On the second serve, the two players were in a battle of superiority. Thomas again rushed the net and stopped Catalina in her tracks with a sideways hit to stay in the game. The score was tied 15/15. Thomas kept the pressure on Catalina's forehand and scored again. Catalina was behind 15/30. Austin sat quietly in his seat in a paralyzed state; Catalina was on her own. Catalina hit the net twice in a row giving, Thomas the advantage of 15/40. Catalina knew she had to block out the pain to win, her next serve rifled in at 101 mph, blowing past Thomas like a bullet. 30/40.

"Wow," said Austin, "That serve came out of nowhere."

Catalina eyed Thomas with the look of self-reliance. Giving it her all, and then some, she aced Thomas to tie the score 40/40. Catalina's next serve clocked at 98mph. Thomas hit the net; 40/30. Catalina's actions mesmerized everyone in the crowd; this doesn't happen to a long shot with a hurt arm. Catalina eyed Austin for the last time; she said a prayer under her breath and unleashed her serve; Thomas returned the ball uniformly in Catalina's direction. Nine squares appeared in Catalina's eyes. She needed Thomas to enter square 6. Catalina hit her mark, Thomas retrieved the ball from square 6, Cat saw her opening for the win, all she had to do is hit square 4. With two hands on the racket, she gave it her all, hitting the line on square 4 to win the game and the set. Catalina raised her index finger into the air and pointed it towards God. Austin jumps up with joy, then hugged Savanna. Catalina won the tournament. Cat ran and jumped into Austin's arms with tears of satisfaction rolling down her cheeks.

As Catalina received her trophy, he could see the crowd was falling in love with her. Austin cried with joy while holding Savanna in his arms, he knew she was unique, and he knew the hard work was beginning.

CHAPTER 18

Two weeks later, Catalina sat on Austin's couch; her arm was still in a cloth sling. She just came back from physical therapy. Austin walked into the room, holding an excellent cup of coffee. "How's treatment going?"

"In another six weeks, I'll be good to go."

"The U.S. Open is in six weeks," said Austin. "By the way, the results of the wild card came in today. I'm sorry to tell you this." Austin hesitated with his head down. "You're in."

Catalina jumps up with emotions not seen by most people. Savanna entered the room with a celebration cake that read, *U.S. Open, here we come.* Catalina threw off the sling. "I'm ready!"

"What happened to six weeks?" said Austin.

"April fools," said Cat. "Therapy releases me today. Let's cut the cake; I'm hungry," yelled out Cat.

∷

As Cat made her way out the front door an hour after her arrival, Austin told her, "Training starts tomorrow, eight o'clock shape, and don't be late!"

Her glow on her face was brighter than the sun. "See you at eight."

∷

Later that evening, Savanna heard the doorbell. When she opened the door, Grace was standing on the porch. "Hi Grace, welcome back; I'll get the coach, come on in, and have a seat."

Austin entered the room with a warm smile from his heart; he wasn't shocked to see her. "How are things in your life going?" said Austin.

"All good, I heard about Catalina's win." Austin could feel her forgiveness from her inner soul; her beautiful face turned into dark clouds as a tear of forgiveness flooded her face. "I'm sorry," said Grace.

Austin reaches for her hand, pulls her up, and gave her a bear-like hug. The clouds burst open. He patted her on the back. As the tears were drying, Austin said, "I need your help to train Catalina."

"It would be my honor."

Austin smiles back. "Before you leave, you have to have some cake." As if she was listening, Savanna walked out, holding two pieces of strawberry cake.

Austin was sitting on the aluminum bench next to the tennis court, sipping on his vanilla Frappuccino with two shots of espresso. Catalina rode in on a man's bike. "Good morning coach," said Catalina.

"Good morning." Austin noticed another bike rider approaching from the other side of the park. Catalina also noticed, Catalina quickly realizes its Grace. They watched in silence as Grace slammed on her brakes right in front of the bench.

Catalina expressed her thoughts with the coach. "What is she doing here?"

"Catalina, this is Grace, Grace, this is Catalina."

All three bust out laughing. "Seriously," said Cat. "Why is she here?"

"I'm here to help you win," said Grace.

Catalina stares at Austin, then said, "I'm good with that outcome," as both girls smiled.

Austin told both of them to have a seat. Austin had been waiting his whole life for this day. Austin's speech pulled out from the draws of his mind. "The U.S. Open is the world's most challenging tennis tournament; it has broken thousands of players; on the glass is a half-full theory, your heartbeat is also your greatest strength; you have to find courage from within. Use prayer for help from above. One hundred twenty-eight of the world's best players. Catalina, you have 7 rounds of tennis in a two-week time frame. We need to work on endurance and nine squares. If you're not up for the task now, it's time to speak up."

Grace eyed Catalina and said, "I think he's been watching too many *Rocky* movies." Both girls laughed uncontrollably.

Austin said, "That was good. We need to build those legs into tree trunks. Lets start with a lap around the park."

The girls took off running as Austin sipped on his Frappuccino and laughed. Austin got out his notepad, which had his plan of action written down. Number one, his exercise plan would include sit-ups, weight lifting, swimming, biking, pull-ups, jogging, and of course, tennis. Number two, on the paper he has written nine squares, he pulls out the sketch from his office. His face was like a picture; in a photograph, signs of faith shined off the image.

Grace and Catalina were finishing warming up. Austin walked over to talk about nine squares. He looked over towards Grace and said, "I think three more weeks she'll be ready, after that will be out of time."

Everybody on the court yelled, "Austin!"

The girls laid their tennis rackets on the court. When you play nine squares, its-a a mental game.

"No rackets," Catalina yelled.

Austin stood in square 2; Grace in square 8.

"Those are the most used squares in the game," said Austin. "From those two squares, they'll determine the outcome of the game. The outside squares are your final destination. You want the other player confused. If Grace is on eight, Catalina's goal is to push her opponent's on square 4 or square 6, then aim for the opposite side. If you are on the squares in front of the net, if you can't hit squares 1, 3 from the net, your opponent has a 70% chance of beating you. If you run for the net, you better be 100% sure."

After six hours of practicing nine squares, the girls looked like tennis zombies. Walking past the coach, holding their hands and arms stretched forward, looking like zombies, they headed straight for their bikes, leaving coach all alone.

CHAPTER 19

It was the last Saturday in August, two days away from the start of the U.S. Open.
Austin was sitting on the front porch drinking a refreshing glass of flavored water. Savanna entered the outside from the screen door and sat down. "How's the packing going?"

"Finished two weeks' worth of clothes, four suitcases. And three of them are yours."

"Do you think she can win?" said Savanna.

"I think she can build her confidence right out of the gate with a first round win. The real question is, when she receives her first beating, can she bounce back? Nine squares has to beat out experience," said Austin.

Savanna's cheerful voice said, "She has the best instructor."

Austin smiled. Savanna kissed him with her lips, then walked inside. Austin sat down as he speculated on nine squares.

Arriving at the hotel Sunday afternoon, Austin's three angels were with him. Having two adjoining rooms kept the girls from wandering; New York is a big city.

Monday in New York was a photo opportunity, a picture-perfect day. At the stadium, winds were blowing from the east at five mph, a smoking hot day. Entering the tennis center parking lot was a memorable moment. The girls were panting as their faces were sticking through the open windows, trying to take it all in. Believing was hard to swallow. Austin and the girls were walking past the largest stadium, Arthur Ashe. Austin was planting a seed of victory. "It would help if you saw yourself, in that stadium in two weeks, with a full crowd that's calling your name," said Austin. "Have a seat, ladies. I'm going to register to get our program; I'll be right back." Walking out of sight, he pulled out his notepad and crossed out things to do. Number one on his list of phrases was: you must envision your win.

Austin arrived thirty minutes later with water drinks in hand. Austin revealed the schedule for the first round, which started at one o'clock. The countdown was one hundred and twenty minutes. Austin and the girls transported themselves to the practice courts.

"Grace!" said Austin, "Give Catalina a slow warm-up, in the same way, you would play at the beach with a beach ball, popping it back and forth."

Grace hit a soft serve over the net. Catalina slammed it with all her energy in front of square seven. Catalina raised both arms and yelled out, "Scores!"

Austin eyes Savanna and said, "Sometimes she drives me crazy."

Savanna laughed. "You have to let her have some fun, or she'll hate what she's doing."

After 30 minutes of warm-up, the girls sat under the tree of life in the shade; refueling was taking place.

"Catalina!" yelled out Austin. "Go to the locker room and get dressed. Meet us back at the court," he said as he and Grace disappeared in the shadows of light.

Catalina entered the arena wearing a vibrant fluorescent blue tennis outfit. Savanna said, "She looks like a Christmas bulb with legs."

Austin laughed, then shook his head sideways. Catalina and Grace were practicing warming up for the first game. Across the arena, a flickering light had Austin's attention. It was a timed clock reading fourteen minutes until game time. His nerves started to tingle. Before the match began, all three warm bodies had a huddle. Silence came from the girls as Austin was giving instructions. "After the Second return shot, start nine squares if you wait for a third rally, which leaves the door open for your opponent to set up a shot. That's what we need to avoid. Are we clear?" said Austin.

"As clear as a window," responded Catalina.

"If we can get her to chase nine squares, she's toast. I need you to keep up a fast pace, don't let her breathe; you can do it; I'm proud of you," said Austin.

Catalina patted her heart, with her fist closed, her other hand was pointing towards heaven. She turns around, then walked onto the court. Catalina's first opponent was Patty Defino, a student at Delaware State University. Her family was labeled the well to do of society. Half her life has been inside a tennis club; she was well trained.

In the announcer's booth was a young man whose coworkers called him Rhett Young. He was twenty-one years old and a very handsome young man. Formerly a tennis guru who blew his knee into dust, ending his tennis career. He was studying the announcement schedule. One hundred twenty-eight players are fighting for the title. It's the only sport in the world that a nobody can become somebody in two weeks. He was flipping through the stats trying to find anything on Catalina's match. "She is a ghost in the world of tennis," mumbled Rhett.

Austin was giving his last bit of instructions and a pep talk to Catalina. Catalina was ready to pound some yellow balls. During the coin toss, Catalina heard the negative news; Defino would serve first. The air felt thick with anticipation—two young talented players. One of them will have problems sleeping tonight, and the other one will sleep like a baby.

Catalina was wobbling back and forth, showing her readiness. Patty forced the ball into Catalina's racket with the power of a lightning strike. The ball blew past Catalina for the point. 15/love. Catalina regained her self-control, waited for the second shot, then rushed the net to set up nine squares; with a baby hit on square 3, Patty failed to reach the ball. The score was tied 15/15. The goal was to keep Patty out of breath by keeping her running up and down the court, trying to get impossible shots. Catalina again struck back with a line shot on square 6. After that point, Catalina knew Patty wasn't the fastest runner from the starting gate. Catalina led 15/30.

Patty rebounded with a line shot from the first serve; the score was 30/30. Catalina worked nine squares into the game, set it up, hit it out of bounds. Patty had the advantage of 40/30. An ace jumped past Catalina; Patty took the first game.

Sitting dumbfounded in his soft ergonomic chair, Rhett went over the stats one more time. Locking down from the sports box, he thought to himself, he was expecting better.

Every team has a huddle section. Huddles have won more games than any other player. "You could win this match," said Austin.

Catalina agreed. "OK."

The great thing about huddles is, everybody has to agree with the coach. Catalina may be part of a team, but she's all alone when she's on the court. A different Catalina walked across the court; a dream stealer was in front of her. Even with a headwind, she pushed the limits on each serve, setting up nine squares from every angle; Patty's physical destruction took place as a theory tightened its grab. Catalina beat her easily in two straight sets. The crowd exploded like a fireworks show. After shaking hands with her opponent, that meant thank you for letting me defeat you. Catalina smiled as if she just received her first Christmas gift. Then she jumped in the air and floated with joy. The four of them held hands well, imitating ring around the rosy. Rhett stood up and watched this small moment in time. He remembered the childhood game, laughing out loud.

The group were practicing dinner habits and celebrating Catalina's first win. Austin gave a toast to the three girls in his life, who's blessing has runneth over. Closing his support bars on his lips, he sat down. After eating a piece of bread, his lips opened again. "Catalina and Grace, good work! How did nine squares feel?"

"For the most part, good, only a couple of times I spaced out, got confused, I was saved by the net, twice. Who's on the list for tomorrow?"

"Don't worry about it, I'll tell you tomorrow. When you're finished with dinner, you can head back to the room and get some rest. Your tournament starts at 10 o'clock. It would help if you were fresh. Get some rest," said Austin.

CHAPTER 20

Arriving at the stadium, Austin could hear the noise coming from the stands. "There are probably 5000 people in the stands," said Austin. His thoughts had him looking through a clean window. Catalina was in the center of the window on the outside. Austin's eyes became his mind while his mind turned off.

"Your next victim is Meja Carnell from Sweden. She's ranked 53 in the world. Remember, nine will beat out experience every time if you apply it," said coach, with his eyebrows raised high. "I have something to do. I'll be back in an hour. Warm Catalina up, Grace, don't wear her out," smiled Austin.

Austin disappeared into the crowd, then headed in the direction to view a game played in Arthur Ashe stadium. The number one player in the world was now playing in her second round. Austin found a seat high in the grandstands. Vivian Green, twenty-nine years old and the number one player in the world. She'd had a great year, for her opponents, not so good. Vivian had won the first set and was on her way to winning the second. Austin's inner thoughts were in the playbook of tennis. His job was to keep Catalina's sights off of Vivian. There's enough to worry about today, so why worry about Vivian.

Catalina was standing in the middle of the court wearing a light fluorescent purple tennis outfit, plum color. Austin giggled from looking at her dress. Catalina called out heads for the coin toss; again, she lost. Carnell served first.

Austin and the gang were sitting down waiting for the start of the match. Carnell's first serve was a definite hit, lined up in front of Catalina. Catalina's return hit the net. Carnell scored the first point. 15/love. Grace reassured the coach, "It always takes Catalina a few swings to warm up."

On the second serve, Catalina reached and pulls out nine squares. She backhanded the ball toward square 6; she watched Carnell race in the direction of the ball. *Perfect,* thought Catalina, as she grabbed hold of Carnell's return and annihilated it on square 4 for the win. 15/15. Grace smiled, then said, "See what I mean? Put a hundred dollars on Catalina for me."

Savanna and Austin cracked up laughing. Carnell's next line shot aced the white line for the win. 30/15. Catalina's return percentage had to be higher; if not, nine squares would be impossible to set up. Catalina retracted a little, waiting to set up nine squares; she began her attack toward the net, blocking a hard-hit shot, the ball rolled on square 3. Carnell had no choice but to retreat. 30/30. As Catalina became friends with the net, Carnell's talents started to erode. Carnell overpowered her serve; Catalina pulled back her racket from a full swing and observed the outer bounds. Catalina took the lead 30/40.

After Carnell hit a perfect serve, Catalina rushed the net after the first stroke, trying to stop the return. She stretched her left arm and successfully defended her side of the court, the ball dropped on Carnell's side of the net. The first game was over, Catalina had taken the early lead.

Catalina started playing like a ping pong player at the world finals, ponging shots with spins and speed. She was chopping down her opponent like a tree ready to fall. Nine squares were working like a tremendous machine. Catalina was scoring at will, as her opponent was spinning like a merry-go-round. Catalina won the first set, six games to two.

During the time out, Austin sent Grace to chat with Catalina. From a distance, Austin could see the girls laughing. Grace returned to her seat a few minutes later. Austin questioned her on her pep talk. "What did you say to her?" asked Austin.

Grace responded, "I asked her what kind of dessert is she having for dinner." Savanna and Austin had confusing appearances. "I told her if she wins, I'll buy dessert."

"That's your pep talk," said Austin.

"Yep," said Grace.

The second set began much differently. Catalina ran from the gate like a thoroughbred and took the lead, and never looked back. She won the next set of six games to one, Catalina advanced to the round of 32.

Using his feet as a backup motor to pull out his chair, Rhett stood up. "I can't believe what I just saw. Wow." He grabbed his briefcase and headed for the door.

Catalina signed autographs for over an hour. Grace had to pull her away; it was time to go home. On the car ride back to the hotel, Austin started giggling and it got contagious. Nobody knew why, they were laughing. Finally, Austin spoke out, he said, "Catalina! You just won 100,000 dollars!" and started laughing.

Catalina screamed out, "We're millionaires!"

Grace said, "Not even close."

"It's a million to me, so let me dream."

"Two out of seven wins," said Savanna, the whole table clapped. Dinner had champagne, and cokes for the girls, the drink of champions, celebrating not just for the win but also for the hard work that was starting to pay off. Nine squares were the real winner. The four of them were finishing dinner next to the hotel. They were sharing memories from the match and laughing at her opponent's faces as she walked off the court.

"Good night, ladies," said Austin. "I'm heading to bed, it's been a long day. See you in the morning."

Savanna and the girls talked for a while before closing down the night.

CHAPTER 21

The Catalina fashion show was now taking place. Wednesday was Catalina's day off; she and Grace were shopping in New York, looking for new tennis outfits, and running around Central Park, acting like teenagers.

Labor Day weekend temperatures are reaching 102 degrees, with humidity at 99. Austin was sitting in their room close to the air conditioner. In front of his nose were stacks of files. "What are you searching for?" said Savanna.

"Autumn Anderson, our next player."

"You have files on all the players?" said Savanna.

Austin grinned, his lips spit out the word, "Yes."

"Even the number one seed?"

Austin laughed. "Yes. Each player has a weakness. It may not be noticeable to the average person; we need all the advantages we can find. The next five opponents are the best players in the world."

"Do you still think she has a chance?" said Savanna. "We're come a long way from hitting balls in the snow."

"Whether we win or not, we've achieved a lot in eight months. And yes, I still think she can win," said Austin.

Catalina and Grace were sitting in their hotel room, watching the number one seed dismantling her opponent last night in straight sets. Silence filled the air. Grace's heart skipped a beat, wondering what would happen if Catalina reached the finals against the number one seed. Negative words entered Grace's skull. Grace slowly pressed delete.

Thursday morning was a gorgeous day in New York; four days had disappeared from the calendar, along with two opponents. Catalina's next match started at 6:00 pm. Catalina's next opponent was a 27-year-old named Autumn Anderson. She turned pro four years ago, after college. She was ranked 25th in the world. The only headache she'd had so far has been for her opponents. She had won all her matches; she would be tough to beat.

Arriving at 4:30 pm, Catalina was headed to the dressing rooms while Savanna and Austin and Grace were on the way to the grandstands. Austin's head turned at the neck. He was seeing Catalina signing autographs. His heart melted like butter that was boiling in water. His little prodigy is growing up and becoming famous.

Rhett Young walked into the announcer's box, wearing all white and holding a briefcase in his left hand. Sitting at his desk Rhett opened up his files. "Autumn Anderson," said Rhett. "She's ranked 25 in the world, age 27. No grand slams titles under her belt; last year, she was ranked 49th." Rhett opened the next folder. "Catalina, no ranking, 15 years old, in her first tournament, and she's not even on her high school tennis team."

Rhett's co-worker walked in, his assistant John. "It feels like an easy match for Autumn; the girl she's playing is a nobody. She's lucky to get this far," said John.

"That may be true, but she's beat two opponents in straight sets. How do you explain that?" said Rhett.

"You can't."

"If she wins, I'm going to talk to her, see if I can find out how she's winning."

"Good luck with that one," said John.

Rhett turned his chair around and looked down towards the tennis court; his mind almost went blank. Then he says two words, "Good luck."

Grace and Catalina entered the stadium. Catalina was wearing another bright outfit, a fluorescent red with matching socks that you could probably see from space. The sun was setting while Grace was exercising Catalina. Austin walked out to the court and met up with Catalina and Grace to discuss the match. "How do you feel?" asked Austin.

"Never better," responded Catalina.

Austin had Catalina focus on Autumn as she warmed up. "When things don't go her way, she gets frustrated and loses momentum. We don't want a rally race; keep setting up nine squares, which in its self should frustrate her."

The girls hi-fived Austin with their tennis rackets against his flat hand, which indicates their belief in victory.

"Rhett!" said John. "We have ten minutes to game time; what are you doing?"

"Have you seen the stats on Catalina?" said Rhett, "The 15-year-old? She wins the qualifying tournament to get into the U.S. Open. It was her first tournament. She wins the tournament, then wins the lottery. She beats the four of the best players in qualifying. Her serves clocked at over 104 MPH. Her coach is a retired high school tennis coach and she's in the round of 32, unbelievable. This game will be a real test," said Rhett, as he grabbed the mic and said, "It's game time!" over the loudspeakers.

The sound of "Good evening," burst from the loudspeakers. "We have a sellout crowd for tonight for a round of 32 match between the 25 seed Autumn Anderson and Catalina Davis."

Hearing the announcer's sounds that we have a sellout, Catalina had the same feeling from opening a Christmas present.

The coin toss goes back as far as the Romans; we now call it heads and tails; then, it was called ships and heads. Because ships were on the coins, and Pompey the Great, his head was on the other side. Autumn won the toss, it's heads. Autumn spun the ball straight towards Catalina. Autumn hadn't realized yet, but she would. She just served into Catalina's sweet spot. Catalina aimed the shot to hit square 9, forcing the game on Autumn. Autumn's legs delivered a full stretch; somehow, she returned it. Catalina locked on squares 4 or 7. Catalina over-hit the ball, it went out of bounds, 15/love. The second serve landed an inch from the back centerline. Catalina sought out nine squares with a soft hit that seemed like a traffic jam as it made its way towards square 3. Autumn ran for the shot and hit a hard blow towards Catalina. Catalina popped a high fly over Autumn's head and hit the back of the court for the point. Her shaking left fist told the crowd, I'm here to win. Are you behind me? 15/15. Serve number three. Catalina thought too soon, the net and the enemy become friends. 30/15. Autumn served a powerful forward spinning yellow ball that as well as said goodbye as it blew past Catalina, 40/15. Austin stared over at Grace. Their eyes met, he shook his head back in forth, as to say, I don't know! Catalina returned a low-flying ball that was captured by the net. Autumn had won the first game quickly.

Catalina took a minute break, sipping on a Gatorade as if she was at the world's fair. Austin and Grace arrived at the same time.

"Talk to me?" said Austin.

"She just got some early lucky shots, and that's all," said Cat.

"Keep pushing nine squares and keep Autumn running. You can do it," said Austin. The four most significant positives words someone can say to another person.

Catalina started the game using a canon instead of a racket. Sliding her first shot at 103 mph directly at Autumn, who, much to Catalina's surprise, hit a cheap line shot. Love/15. Autumn pressed on as if she was the winner. She jumped ahead of Catalina's returns; nine wasn't allowed to work. Autumn continued to dominate and win the 2nd game. Catalina watched Autumn serve with accuracy and rushing the net as if there were two players against one; Autumn won the first set 6-0.

Down on the bench, Catalina and Grace were sitting on both sides of the coach. All are staring at their feet. Austin turned towards Catalina and said, "She's outrunning nine. If she's outrunning nine, she's outrunning you." Austin smiles, then said, with love, "Fix the problem."

A double mirror smile, with different faces, with the same common goal, were facing one another. Cat had to win the next three sets in a row to win the match. It had never been done before by a 15-year-old in her first tournament.

In the announcer's booth, Rhett's co-worker John put his fingertips on Rhett's shoulders; sound traveled into Rhett's ear. "I'll bet you a hundred, your darling loses."

Without looking up or back, Rhett's hands go into a handshake.

Thirty-two feet in front of Catalina, there was a young lady, in Catalina's way, thought Catalina. "Game time," yelled out the referee.

Autumn was a fighter, a bulldog with smaller teeth. Catalina became the Doberman in the fight. By winning the next two sets in under an hour.

In the announcement booth, everyone was chattering. You could hear John talking to Rhett. "Two sets, in record time, and she's not even ranked," said John. "We need to tell this story before anyone else does."

"If she wins, I'll catch the first interview," said Rhett. "All she has to do now is win."

All eyes were on the fourth set of a fantastic comeback by a young tennis star. The word spread throughout the tournament and photographers were pouring into the stadium taking pictures of the kid prodigy. The fourth set was the hardest. Each player was leading by a neck. If it were a horse race, it would be a photo finish. Catalina used her whip with four games apiece to turn on the power from within her own body, winning the fifth game from the advantage spot, crossing the finish line first.

Catalina was sweating out the water from her body for the cause of victory. Autumn fired the second return shot from square eight. Catalina's body sped up towards the net, then slowed down for the soft touch; she eyed square three. The image became a reality by searching and seeking its final destination. Autumn wasn't fast enough to reach the front on her side of the court. Love/15. Catalina felt exhausted, thinking back to the skateboard exercise. Catalina needed stamina and strength more than head knowledge. Catalina's serve was on reserve as the rally continues. Autumn fought for survival with a line shot on the court's east side and tied the game 15/15. Catalina's first serve entered the net. Her second serve slowed to a crawl, allowing Autumn to stay ahead of nine squares, winning a rally of eight to take the lead. 15/30. Catalina looked towards heaven, then spotted the yellow ball slipping downward. Her right arm attached to her racket hit a line drive directly toward Autumn's feet, throwing her off balance. The ball headed out of bounds. The game was tied 30/30. The rally continued, Catalina opening up nine squares to full capacity. She eyed square 6 with a backhand. Autumn fell for the setup, returned the shot only to be captured by nine squares. Catalina rushed the net and forehanded the ball onto square 4 for the win. 40/30. Austin was crossing his fingers. One more point for success. Grace squeezed Savanna's hand. Catalina's eyes had the look of a cougar, right before its prey would become dinner. Catalina rushed the net during Autumn's return and stopped the ball in its tracks, landing on square 2 for the win. Cat fell to her knees, while her face had tears of joy.

She fell backward. The stadium erupted like a volcano. Grace jumped with joy and ran down to congratulate Catalina; Austin grabbed Savanna's hand and pulled her out of her seat. They rushed in Catalina's direction; he hugged Catalina. Tears rained from his face. "I'm proud of you. Nine squares were in full swing. By the end of the match, Autumn knew Catalina was unique. Three straight sets to win the game."

John walked into Rhetts booth and handed him a hundred-dollar bill. "I think we're on to something, Did you see that?" said John. "We have fifteen-year-old in the top sixteen players."

Rhett had to find out what made this girl tick. He headed downstairs to get an interview, hurrying before she left. Rhett slowly disappeared, leaving the lights on.

Hugs, with laughter, tears of gladness, a goal, and God, Catalina, tell the world. She's blessed. Austin released his bear hug and smiled. "I'm impressed. Three straight, but remember we're not out of the woods yet; take a shower. We'll meet you near the car."

Catalina ran into Rhett Young, exiting out of the locker room, holding up a sign that read, *Catalina*.

"Can I help you?" said Catalina.

"I want to interview you if you have a few minutes. By the way, my name is Rhett Young."

"Pleased to meet you, Mr. Young."

They both broke out laughing. "On not such a serious note, where did you learn how to play tennis?" said Rhett.

"In the park," said Catalina. Rhett looked a little bewildered. "That's when I met coach Austin. I was playing tennis in the park last year in the snow."

"In the snow," said Rhett with a puzzled voice.

"I was playing tennis in the snow when the coach spotted me," said Catalina.

Rhett still couldn't wrap his head around the snow and tennis. He continued with his questions. "Let me understand what you're saying; you've only been playing for a year, and you started by playing in the snow?"

Catalina laughed, then said, "That's right."

"Did you play in any other tournaments?" said Rhett.

Catalina said, "My first tournament was the qualifying tournament to get into the U.S. Open. Then I won the wild card. God is good," said Catalina.

"What's your secret?" said Rhett.

"Nine squares are the secret weapon," It just flowed out of her mouth like Niagara Falls.

"What're nine squares?" questioned Rhett.

Catalina heard Grace yelling from the car, "Let's go."

"Got to go," said Catalina as she ran off, leaving Rhett thinking.

On the way back to the hotel, Austin again started to giggle. He said, "The quarter-finals just paid $163,000. Can we get a cheer? Noise excitement is always complementary medicine. Sleep in tomorrow. We have a day off, while practice in the evening gets some rest."

CHAPTER 22

Austin was sitting in his hotel room with his laptop on his lap. Austin was online reading the news. On the news front, all the sports pages read the same thing. There was a new darling on the tennis court. A fifteen-year-old sensation in her first tournament reaches round sixteen in the U.S. Open. Austin knew her fame would rise, but not so quickly.

Upstairs, along the stadium's front side, the windows reflected the natural light from the sun. Inside was the sports center, a control room, with empty chairs. Rhett walked in, sat down, and looked through the shiny glass. The room awakened as the staff started to fill the space. John settled in next to Rhett. "Good afternoon," said John.

Rhett smiles then drinks his coffee. "Is the world ready to see their new tennis star?" Rhett said to John.

"Let's see what she has in her tank tonight; her opponent is ranked 11 in world rankings. She was runner up in the French Open; her name is Sofia Maroni. Twenty-four, well trained and hungry."

Rhett looks over at John and said, "Have you heard of something called nine squares, referring to tennis?"

"I've never heard of it," said, John. "Why?"

"Nothing, don't worry about it," replied Rhett.

Catalina and Grace were ten steps ahead of Savanna and Austin walking into the stadium. The sun was setting; walk lights were popping on. Savanna asked who she was playing tonight.

"Sofia Maroni," said Austin. "Ranked 11th."

In other words, Catalina was going to have to upshift to win.

Entering the stadium was a sight for anyone's eyes, a packed house full of reporters from the news stations. All wanted to see and touch their new story—a fifteen-year-old tennis sensation named Catalina Davis. Austin circled Catalina with Savanna and Grace locked in arms. The reporters were blocking them similarly to a wall surrounding a fort. Questions flowed in from all sides. Austin said, "No questions at this time, please."

Austin rushed Catalina towards the dressing room, a haven. Austin was next in line for questions from the reporters. "Is it true? Is this her first tournament?" said one of the reporters.

"Yes, that's right. No further questions please, I have to prepare for the match. When Catalina wins, I'll answer a few more questions," said Austin.

Hearing the crowd clap, Grace and Austin turned around to see what the fuss was. Catalina skipped from the locker room, wearing her bright yellow outfit onto the court. She was the fashion queen. Standing in the center of the court, Austin was talking to Grace and Catalina. It was hard for the girls to pay attention; they couldn't help themselves; watching the crowd expand was similar to a balloon filling with air. "You just had to watch." Austin pulled the girls back into his train of thought by his lips. "Listen up," he said. "The good news is we're in the round of 16, and the bad news is, Sofia Maroni showed up tonight." Austin laughed. "I was hoping she wouldn't show up. The good news is she going to lose tonight. Do we all agree?"

All hands and tennis rackets went into the famous center handshake.

Austin could see something wasn't right with Catalina. "Please speak to me! What's wrong?" said Austin.

"I don't feel like playing tonight," said Cat. Austin's eyes shrank into a black hole. Grace and Catalina detected a motionless coach that didn't know what that meant. The top of his head was about to blow off. Cat yelled out, "Gotcha!"

Grace applauded, and then said, "Coach, you need to have a good time. Cat and I will figure this out, now take your seat." She yelled out, "Relax!" as Austin walked off. Grace faced Catalina and said, "Beat this girl." Two twin laughs exploded uncontrollably, causing a scene.

Catalina headed for the court. Grace walks to her seat. Catalina received the first break, a winning coin toss for the first time with heads. All eyes were watching the Chanel of Catalina. The stadium was quiet; commercials would have to wait. Catalina used anger with confidence to create her masterpiece. Grunting during the serve sounded like two dogs playing tug a war with a long rope. Eventually, one will back off. After the third rally, it was more than enough time to set up nine squares. Catalina aimed for square 6, hoping for a return. Sofia lost her footing, stumbled, and smacked the ball into the net. 15/love. According to the coach, Sofia had trouble hitting balls over one hundred mph. Whether Catalina went out or won this round is a lot of stress for a fifteen-year-old. The battle continued on the court, Sofia wasn't going home, and Catalina wasn't quitting. Their rally seemed to be with swords instead of rackets. The crowd became mesmerized; their heads went back and forth. Sofia won the first set with advantages. Austin was upset. "What are you doing there?" said Austin.

"Playing tennis!" said Catalina. "That's what we're here for."

"One set down is not a laughing matter. You're one set away from going home. I guess we can't hide from the truth. She's better than you."

Grace couldn't believe Austin just said what he said. Catalina grabbed her racket from Austin's hand and walked off. Austin returned to his seat. Savanna said, "What happened down there?"

His response was watch. Austin hoped his words would not backfire; it was time for Catalina to turn pro. Grace overheard the conversation; Catalina needed a swift kick. Catalina wiped the tears from her eyes. Her first serve reached unprecedented speeds of 106 mph. Sofia couldn't handle anger; Catalina took the first point 15/love. Her second serve hit the net. A slow second shot could mean disaster. If she hit the net or Sofia found a clean shot, either way, she could lose. Her second serve hit the line. The radar lit up; it read 107 mph. Sofia swung late, the ball went out of bounds. 30/love. Sofia's return was on the attack with a perfect backhand landing on the outside line 30/15. She repeated the same attack on the next serve, 30/30. Sofia gained confidence by attacking the net, stopping her younger opponent from winning the point 30/40. Catalina threw her entire body into the serve. The radar clock read 106 mph, acing Sofia, and tied the score 40/40. Catalina grunted her next serve for her second ace in a row; Catalina now had the advantage. And for the third time, she backed it up with a blistering serve, reaching 107 mph; Sofia slammed the yellow ball into the net. Catalina won the game. Rhett's head turned, John faced Rhett. Unbelievable just became believable. Catalina muscles expanded to the point of breaking. Across the net, Sofia couldn't keep up with Cat's serve or nine squares. The plan was working, and nine squares were boiling. Slow-motion entered the match as Catalina started to apply nine squares on every shot; not only did Cat win the set, but she also won the second set in record time. The game was tied one set apiece.

In the announcer's booth, Rhett was pulling his hair out, thinking about nine squares and how it worked. Rhett took out his binoculars. His focus was on Catalina; sometimes, players talk to themselves as they're hitting the ball. Maybe he'd learn something.

Catalina was on the receiving end. Players sometimes think that's the wrong end. Catalina embraced the situation that was testing her ability. A perfect serve challenged Catalina, who was trying to stay ahead of Sofia with quick responses. Catalina planted the yellow ball in square 7. The roots were weak; Sofia returned the serve. Quickly reacting, Catalina threw down a hit with a downforce curve that landed on square 6. Sofia fails in front of 15,000 people; the score is love/15. The second rally came relatively easy for Catalina as Sofia returned the ball into the net. Love/30. A challenging rally followed, with Cat continuing her takedown comeback; she set up nine squares and rushed to the front of the net, then tapped the yellow ball to square 3. Sofia stood on the rear side of the court, helpless. Sofia's winning streak had come to an end. She served two foul shots into the net, game over. Catalina's turn to perform. Catalina stared deep into Sofia's eyes. Her breathing was heavy; her muscles were losing their protein; Catalina had trained to be automatic with her reactions on the court. She was going to get the job done, regardless. Catalina quickly jumped on top, with a 103 mph powerhouse serve past Sofia's racket. Impressive after two hard sets. 15/ Love.

Up in the announcer's booth, John and Rhett both had their mouths open. Rhett said, "Wow."

Catalina hit again with a 104 mph serve right past Sofia. 30/love. Catalina stared at Grace; Grace stared at Catalina, Grace nodded at square 4 and held up four fingers; for it to work, Catalina would have to hit a deep shot on square 9, rush the net, and send it home from square 4. Catalina served deep toward square 9. Catalina rushed the net as Sofia gave her back the ball. Catalina backhanded the ball with a bullet-like precision with only seconds to react, landing on the outer line of square 4. Sofia took a nasty fall running for the ball. 40/love. The referee called time out. Catalina headed for the bench to quench her thirst. Looking towards the coach, Catalina was surprised; the coach wasn't looking her way. Austin was thinks to himself, if she's going to grow, she needed to wean herself off him. After serving, Catalina hit her sweet spot for nine squares to run. Sofia slammed the ball in the opposite direction, fooling Catalina and scored the point. 40/15. Catalina's arm was feeling like a bag of heavy potatoes. Her racket speed dropped to 92 mph—it favored her opponent. Cat's hard head just got harder. There's always one more burst of energy. Catalina was going with a hard serve. Their eyes made contact; Catalina was breathing heavy. Up went the ball; Catalina's serve clocked at over 103 mph. Sofia swung, the yellow ball flew into the net. Catalina won the second game. Sofia used the upper portion of the court after realizing what Catalina was trying to do, creating a tennis roadblock and winning games three and four. Austin knew it would be a matter of time before someone would figure out how to stop nine squares. Needing a time out, Austin's hands formed a tee, letting Catalina know he wanted her to call time. Grace met Austin on the court. Austin said, "I need you to set up nine squares on the first return that would allow you to take back the advantage."

Catalina eyed Grace, and then told her to listen to him; he's paying for the room. Austin stares down Grace with one eyebrow lifted. Catalina and Grace laughed.

"I'd tell you good luck, but luck won't get it done," said Austin. "It has to come from the heart."

The time clock restarted when Sofia started game five, from square 7 with a hard serve. Catalina's first shot opened the door for victory, hitting square 9 on the line, then bounded into the ball girl's hands. Love/15. Catalina continued using nine squares with line shots to win four straight times to win the next game. Her accuracy was breathtaking. Catalina gained control and confidence, which is a state of mind. Every minute of every serve, Catalina's racket took apart Sofia's game and put it back in the box. Catalina won the set 6 games to 2. Catalina dropped her racket and then threw her ten fingers into the air; she moved on to the quarterfinals.

In the car heading to the hotel, Catalina and Grace never shut up. Austin and Savanna giggled in the front seat. Savanna said, "Do you know how much money you made tonight?"

Savanna yelled out, "250,000 dollars!" A faked, fainting spell in the back seat was followed by the two teenagers started screaming with excitement. It felt good to be excited again, thought Austin. It's sad when we lose it.

CHAPTER 23

Austin was reading the sports news on his iPad while drinking his third cup of coffee.
Austin learned what the media had to say about Catalina. He was reading an
article written by Rhett Young, who announced at the U.S. Open. His report
said Catalina was the best fifteen-year-old in the country with no experience.
His main question in the article was, what's the system called nine squares?
Whatever it is, she's winning with it.

Austin started to get upset. He said, "She told someone." He paid his bill
and headed straight for Catalina's room.

Meeting Savanna in the hallway, she said, "Where are you going?"

"The announcer at the stadium, Rhett Young, writes a column for online
sports. He mentioned a system called nine squares that Catalina is using to
win."

"She slipped, but probably not on purpose," said Savanna. "She is on a
high note, so let it go. If you go in there and yell at her, it's over. Don't crush her
emotions. Go in there with passion and love, and kindly say, we have to watch
what we say." Savanna kissed him on the cheek. "See you after breakfast."

Austin read the numbers on the door, room 525. He knocked harder
than average; loud sounds echoed in the hallway as he stood still waiting for
the door to open. The door separated from the frame. Austin walked right

into the room, Catalina was sleeping, and Grace crawled back in bed, trying to go back to sleep. He sat down on Catalina's bed; his inner thoughts were that of a father protecting his children. Both girls were asleep in their nest. His pep talk would have to wait. He headed back to his room.

Two hours later, the four of them were sitting in the middle of the café. The girls were finishing up breakfast and messing around and acting stupid like two 15-year-olds without knowing how big the U.S. Open will affect their lives.

"Stacy Fray is your next opponent; she from France. Twenty-six years old, an all-around great player. She's ranked 6th in the world. We're still going to follow the same game plan. Hard serves when we have the ball. Then set up nine squares. Any questions?" asked Austin. Both girls started giggling; Austin looked over at Savanna. "Did I say something funny?" said Austin.

The girls kept laughing. "Never mind," said Grace, "It's the fun of being a kid. You don't have to explain."

"We don't play until tomorrow night," said the coach. "Your day is open; see the city. Dinner is at 5:30; we'll meet you in the restaurant."

"What are the two of you doing today?" asked Catalina.

"Resting," said Austin. "Have fun." Watching the girls walk off, Austin yelled out, "Be careful, see you at dinner."

Savanna and Austin headed to the room.

Hours later, Austin was sitting in the desk chair, flipping through his notes. He saw Savanna was still sleeping soundly. Austin returned to the investigating. He returned to his files on all the players. Telling himself, every player has a fault, including Catalina. Flipping down through the files, he stops at the name Vivian Green, the world's number one player. She was playing that night, at eight o'clock. *We need to be at that game*, thought Austin. Catalina needs to see her in action. If we make it that far; that's who she'll face. Speaking quietly to himself, he said, "Vivian has won every set so far, a perfect record going into her fifth match. If she wins the U.S. Open, it will be her third grand slam title this year; she is unstoppable."

Austin and the girls were intrigued to watch Vivian Green, the world's number one player, in her quarterfinals match. As they entered Arthur Ashe Stadium, some girls in the grandstands spotted Catalina and ran down the bleachers making a scene trying to receive an autograph. Twenty-five thousand spectators, fifty thousand eyes turned in that direction. A massive crowd surrounded the four of them. Austin and Savanna slipped under the radar as nobodies and headed for their seats. Catalina started signing autographs with Grace playing her bodyguard. Down on the court warming up, Vivian noticed all the commotion from the south side of the stadium, taking away her fame. She finally figured it out; that's the fifteen-year-old tennis player named Catalina who is causing all the ruckus.

John quickly got Rhett's attention inside the glass tower. "Your girl's here," said John. Rhett looked bewildered; his mind was on Vivian Green's match. "Look out the window to the right," said John.

He saw hundreds of people standing in line for an autograph from Catalina. Rhett glanced on the court and saw Vivian standing by herself, staring at the crowd, and then walking off to prepare for her match. The look on Vivian's face said the golden girl was going to pay for stealing her glory.

Austin nudges Savanna. "Did you see the look on Vivian's face? That's what I was looking for: doubt."

As the game was about to start, Catalina joined them, sitting down on the cheap plastic red seats. Catalina was rubbing her right hand. It was a little sore from signing autographs. "Is your hand ok, honey?" asked Savanna.

"It's ok; it's a bit cramped from signing autographs."

Austin thought about her writing, and shrugged it off. Vivian won the serve; her opponent was Lisa Higgins, ranked fifth in the world. For the next hour and a half, Catalina and Grace sat on the edge of their seats, calculating every move Vivian performed. Vivian disposed of Lisa as if she was an amateur, beating her in two straight sets. Austin and the girls stepped down from the bleachers only to cross paths right in front of Vivian. Catalina couldn't hold back her excitement. "You were fantastic tonight," said Catalina.

Vivian stopped in front of her, looked her over, and then said, "Thanks, maybe one year you'll get your chance when you grow up." She laughed, and then walked off.

Savanna hugged Catalina. "Don't listen to her."

Austin opens his mouth. "Do listen to her; in the end, she's going to owe you an apology. Let's get out of here."

CHAPTER 24

"You're on television tonight," said Austin.

The girls sounded off with excitement. "When you're on TV, do you get paid more, and by the way, how much do I make if I win tonight?" asked Catalina.

Savanna slipped out numbers unfamiliar to the ears of Catalina and Grace. She said, "425,000 dollars."

Catalina and Grace both pretend to pass out in the car. The silence was a pleasure for about 15 seconds.

Walking into the stadium, Catalina received hundreds of fans, all wanting autographs. Austin handed Catalina her first ballpoint pen for autographs and said, "We'll see you on the court. Goodbye."

Catalina entered the court wearing a bright orange outfit. She had the appearance of a lot attendance parking cars with a flashlight. Grace was warming Catalina's muscles; before a match a critical ingredient that you find in stamina. Grace was stretching out Catalina's legs next to the bench waiting for the game to start. The grandstands were full; the lights were on. Hotdogs and pretzels, were flying everywhere. And for five dollars, you get a coke. Austin sat down next to Catalina. He said, "Kidding aside, her backhand is weak, especially on the deep end of square nine." He gave her a smile and a good luck wink. Then headed back to his seat. Her pep talks have been colorful and right to the point. Grace says, "Beat this girl, and let's get ice cream." She smiled and walks off. Catalina shook her head and laughed.

Rhett was eating his dinner. Onion rings and chili cheese fries waiting for the game to begin. John entered the room through the second door and says to Rhett, "You keep eating like that, and you won't see the age of 30."

Rhett barks it off.

"Are you going with the young girl?" asked John.

"I don't know, it's going to be an exciting match. Stacy is playing some fine tennis," said Rhett.

"I guess while knowing the answer in a few hours," said John.

Catalina lost the coin toss, Stacy would serve first. Stacy watched the yellow ball; she threw it over her head. Her hand-eye coordination had to match the puzzle. The ball cleared the net with an inch to spare. Catalina anticipated a hard shot. A quick reaction from Catalina forced the yellow ball to change direction. It was now heading towards square 9. Stacy's racket grabbed hold of the ball and flung it in the opposite direction. Catalina catapulted her shot directly, targeting square 4. A perfect line shot that was captured by the enemy and returned. The good news was, Stacy was too far off track. Catalina used anger with the heart to control her shot. She backhanded the yellow ball deep. It returned to square 9 for the win. Catalina took the first point, love/15. Austin was writing down the number of squares to see how many times it works or doesn't work. Catalina's return was straight and forceful. Stacy stayed on top of the ball with a beautiful forehand. Catalina again eyed the court for an opening for nine squares. Catalina popped a soft shot hitting the net and rolling to the bottom below. There would be no rescue party. 15/15. Stacy ran faster than Catalina could swing; the yellow ball hit the outer line, it bounced into the wall behind Cat's head. 30/15 Catalina smiled then caught Grace's eyes. At the same time, Grace gave the signal with four fingers and then nine fingers. Cat had to use square 6 to set up square 4, and then set up square 9. Getting Stacy on square 4 wasn't easy; she guarded the net with a warrior stance. Cat received the ball, underreacted, and then hit the net. 40/15. Cat tried to stay focused as she returned Stacy's serve. On the second return, Cat turned on nine squares and fired the ball forward towards square 4. Stacy rushed in to reach the ball; her long arms reach far enough; she not only blocked nine, but her shot went sideways, running along with the net, then lands inside the lines, then bounced out of bounds. Stacy won the first game.

For one and a half hours, the pendulum swayed back and forth. The girls were punishing one another. Catalina was sitting on the bench, trying to catch her breath. The score was tied, one set each. Catalina and Stacy were dueling for the third set, three games apiece. Catalina spiraled the ball; it was heading right for Stacy. She hit a solid shot back at Catalina. Catalina's return hit the net. Love/15. Catalina continued serving; her average speed was down to 91 mph, her arms were tired and her legs hurt. And to make matters worse, she was losing. Stacy ripped another hard shot, trying to throw Catalina off her game; it was working. Catalina was starting to fade; Austin called for a time out. Both sides got a five-minute break. Sitting on the bench next to Catalina, Austin was staring straight ahead; Catalina was silent. Austin breaks the silence and said, "There are three games left; you have to win them all. You're better than her," and he pointeds to the sky. "Thou God, all things are possible. No matter tired you are or how helpless it seems. All you need is the faith of a mustard seed to win this match. God thinks you can do it; I think you can do it; Grace and Savanna believe you can." Austin teared up a little. "Go out there and show us what you're made of. Now. 'Beat this girl,' and let's go home."

Austin got up and headed back to his seat.

Catalina looked down; her legs were dangling under the bench where she was sitting. She looked up; she said, "I guess I have to win three games," and giggled.

Catalina was still struggling; Stacy took a 4-3 lead. Catalina slingshot her return with confidence in Stacy's direction. Stacy had her game face on and was ready for the challenge. Catalina fired back the serve, trying to set up nine squares. She locked on where Stacy was standing: square 8. Catalina went for the nine-shot by attacking the net by adding two more feet using her tennis racket. Stacy looked intimidated by Catalina's approach; her ball was short of going over the net, love/15. Catalina clinched her fist; she just boarded the train heading for momentum. Stacy's serve reached the speed of 103 mph. Stacy's eyes saw trouble and doubt; her return hits the net. Love /30. Catalina kept a fast pace by running Stacy all over the court. Then setting up nine squares and slowly gaining points. Love /40. Stacy was frustrated as Catalina's return blew past her right side and bounced off the line for the win, four games apiece. Catalina continued her come back by keeping the pressure on and winning the next round. Five games to four. All eyes were on Catalina. All tongues were quiet. If Catalina won the next game, she would be the first non-ranking player to advance to the semifinals. Catalina glanced at Grace. Grace was holding up six fingers. After Stacy's serve, Catalina swatted it in Stacy's direction. Stacy's reaction was slow; she hit the ball into the net love/15. Stacy battled with herself and the ball of victory. By winning the next point. 15/15. Catalina had little effect; Stacy won the next rally with a perfect line shot 30/15. Catalina remembered Grace was holding up six fingers. For 6 to work, she needed Stacy on square 7. Catalina eyeballed square 7. She hit her target as if the ball was laser-guided. Stacy ran deep towards square 7. She returned the ball awkwardly. Cat backhanded the yellow ball directly in the path of square 6 for the win. Stacy was wondering what happened. 30/30. Catalina could see and almost hear the thoughts of the people in the grandstands. It was like standing on the edge of a building, and the bystanders were waiting to see if you jump or not. Catalina eyed the coach then nodded her head with only two straight points from a win. Coach knew what she was saying, nine squares. Stacy's arm was putting on the brakes; her serves were barely reaching 97 mph. Her fuel tank was on reserve. Stacy slammed the ball with frustration and anger. Catalina quickly enforced the rule by running in front of the net to distract Stacy and hopefully hit square 2 with a blocked shot. Stacy's return succeeded; it flew past Catalina and exited at the court's rear end, and scored. 40/30.Catalina reflected what coach has always said: don't worry about the score; if you win, the crowd will let you know, never leave the game. Catalina smashed her way into a tie by cramming Stacy's space, causing her to drive the ball into the net. 40/40. Cat now had a fresh start. After serving, she repeated her last actions by running towards the net using her racket as a wall. Stacy also repeated her past performance. It was unsuccessful; Catalina dibbled the ball on square 2; it was Catalina's advantage. The crowd was on their feet. Catalina deliverered the performance of a lifetime, a hard-line shot with a quarter-inch to spare, bouncing out of bounds; Catalina was in the semifinals.

The crowd jumped to their feet while erupting with tears of emotion. Fans were coming out of the stands trying to get an autograph. Grace jumped up and hugged Savanna as the three of them head for the court, trying to get past the crowd. News cameras were flashing in the night sky. Catalina loved signing autographs for the kids and everyone. Still being a kid at heart, she knew the feeling after an hour of waiting for the last signature to be signed. Austin and Savanna grabbed Grace and Catalina for the return trip back to the hotel.

CHAPTER 25

Savanna and Austin were sitting in the hotel dining room, waiting for the girls to join them for a dessert.

"There's nothing like a good cup of coffee," said Austin.

Savanna responded, "How true. Who does Catalina play next?"

"She plays the number 2 seed tomorrow night, Stella Para Jean from Italy; if Catalina wins, she could play Vivian Green for the title if Green wins her semifinal match tonight, and that's expected. I'm more worried about Green than I am about Para Jean. Green has won three majors this year. There's a reason she's number 1; plus, she's more potent than Catalina. Para Jean will be Catalina's most formidable opponent so far. Her ability to make game-saving shots is the best I've seen," said Austin. "She's a real talent."

Savanna said, "Catalina will give you all she has; you need to tell her what to do and how to do it."

Two tennis stars came strolling into the restaurant showing off their beautiful smiles as they took a seat. Savanna passed out the dessert menus. Staring at Catalina, she said, "You look tired,"

"It's been a long day," said Catalina. "Stacy was tough today. Thinking back," Catalina said, "it was fun. By the way, how much is the prize money so far?"

Austin glanced at Savanna. "You tell her, honey."

Savanna said, "You have a check in your name for the amount," she slowed her speech to enhance the announcement. Her voice box spoke through her lips, "425,000 dollars."

Catalina and Grace screamed, not with fear but with excitement. Catalina was so excited she could not stop trembling.

"I can buy my mom a house and a new car. When did it get my money?" asked Catalina.

"When the tournament is over. Remember, we have two matches to go," said Austin. "Your next game is in two days, you're playing Stella Para Jean."

Grace starts laughing. "What kind of name is Para Jean?"

"Italian, and she's no laughing matter," said Austin. "She's ranked 2 in the world. She will be in the finals if we don't stop here; we can't let up. Meet me in the morning on the tennis court outside, 4 am," said Austin.

Grace sounded off, "You meant 4 pm, right?" The girls looked at each other.

Austin's response was, "It's time for bed."

After devouring their deserts, everyone headed off to bed.

The sound of the tennis court lights clicked on, turning night into day. Austin walks over to the bench and has a seat. He glanced at his cell phone; the time was 3:50 am. *It's funny how things circled*, thought Austin. *It's been eight months since I saw a young girl playing tennis in the snow. And now we're here at the U.S Open in the semifinals. God gave me the dream to help Catalina have her plan. That's what you call a true and loving God.* His thoughts became silent. He heard Grace and Catalina in the distance.

"Good morning girls."

Not holding anything back, Grace said, "Do you see the sun? No!" yelled out Grace. "And do you know why, because it's the middle of the night!"

Austin laughed. "Did you know as a trainer, you get ten percent of the purse?"

Grace looks over at Catalina. "Is that true?"

"I've agreed to give both of you ten percent apiece," said Catalina. "I've never had a best friend."

Grace's eyes produced water. "I'll be your best friend if you'll have me," she said.

"A best friend is one who takes their eyes off of themselves; it's better to give than to receive," said Catalina. A shower of tears rained down on their cheeks, as they locked in their friendship with a hug.

Austin tried to shut the tears off by going into training mode. "Set your rackets down; you won't need them, said Austin.

Austin sat in the middle of the court on the ground; Catalina and Grace joined him. "I'm going to be upfront with you," said Austin. "I'm not saying you can't win, but we have the number one and number two player in the world standing in front of us. You have to win with your mind. Nine squares and yourself must become one mind. Grace is going to yell out numbers where the other player is standing. In your mind, you need to set nine squares in motion. Just remember the middle court is useless. The front row and both sides are the targets. Grace, yell out a number," said Austin.

"Six!" said Grace, Catalina answered with the number seven.

"Why seven?" asked Austin. "If you hit within a foot of the line on seven, there's no way she can make it from square six, and the same is for the other side," said Austin. "Please attack the net every other play. One, two, three squares are the short game. We will stay out here and study the combinations of nine squares until you make no mistakes; that's when I'll know your mind is full," said Austin.

The memory banks inside Catalina's mind were slowly charging. Hours seem like days. After five hours, Catalina's mind was ready.

CHAPTER 26

They were driving to the area with the radio off. The only noise to be heard was road noise. Everyone was talking to themselves. Pulling up to the site, flashes started going off. Mics were so thick they could block out the sun circled the car. Catalina grabbed Grace's hand and held on. Grace said, "You have a little bit of a following."

Austin said, "Don't give them two many answers. We have a press conference at 4:00 pm."

Catalina and Grace nodded their heads, and both hopped out of the car.

Rhett Young was hosting the press conference for the semi-finals. The room was packed. Every reporter in the industry wanted to hear the story of this fifteen-year-old tennis sensation. No one in the room cared about Stella Para Jean. Catalina and Grace sat next to Austin at the press table.

The first question was, "How long have you been playing tennis?"

"I started learning tennis eight months ago; until then, I just hit tennis balls into the snow," she turned and smiled at Austin. Catalina laughed. Her wittiness took the crowd to laugher.

The second question was, "Do you think a fifteen-year-old can win the Open in her first tournament?"

"Yes," answered Catalina with a full smile, and the room filled with laughter.

"Your prediction for tonight's match?" said one of the reporters.

Catalina said, "I'll beat her in two straight sets."

Everyone chuckled, except Austin. "Any response from Stella?" asked the reporter.

"Those are big words from a nonprofessional," said Stella. The crowd and reporters were about to hear a verbal war.

Grace got upset; no one talked to her friend in that manner. Grace stood up and said to Stella, "I love what you've done with your hair. How do you get it to come out of your nostrils?"

Catalina, along with Austin, tried not to laugh but couldn't help themselves. Rhett quieted the crowd by talking. "Catalina and Stella, good luck tonight," said Rhett. Catalina's face gleamed with light; she has a crush on Rhett.

Walking in the open air, Austin stopped and looks at Catalina, "You told every reporter inside you'll win in two sets."

"You don't think I can do it?" said Catalina.

Austin faced Catalina. "I think you need to answer your question. If you lose, no one is going to take you seriously. I'll meet the two of you on the court."

Savanna was sitting in the trainer's seats, waiting for her husband to appear. Austin walked up from behind and sat down. Savanna noticed the unhappy look on her husband's face. "Did something go wrong at the press conference?"

Laugher poured all over Austin's face. He said, "Catalina told the reporters that she would win in two sets." Savanna and Austin start laughing hysterically.

"Do you think she can do it?" said Savanna.

"Let's say I hope her game matches the size of her head, because it's swollen."

Grace and Catalina come into view. Catalina was wearing a fluorescent green outfit. Grace headed for the seat; Catalina made her way on the court to warm up. Stella was already on the court doing warm-ups. The grandstands were on the path to capacity. Photographers were setting up; overhead lights started glowing.

The judge activated the coin toss; Catalina would serve first. If Catalina had only learned one thing, it was that you need to jump on your opponent and drive the fear of losing under their skin from the start. Catalina's first serve flew over the net at a blistering speed of 106 mph. Stella was in trouble before the ball lifted Catalina's hand. It sliced the backline for the point. The crowd came alive with a high-level cheer. Grace was anxious to see nine squares in play as Catalina continued to win the battle without it. Catalina took the early lead, winning the first game. Austin eyed Grace.

"Did you see 'nine' in that at all?"

"No," answered Grace, "Not one single time. Catalina is trying to win without nine."

Stella forced a hard shot directly at Catalina; she returned the ball on Stella's front side. The ball bounced back in forth between the two as if it was in a marathon. Catalina was trying to wear out her opponent. It was like arm wrestling yourself; there's never a winner until one arm gets tired. Stella won the marathon 15/love. Stella's serve zeroed in at more than 102 mph. Catalina passed the ball to her opponent. Stella gave it back to Catalina. She backhanded the yellow object towards the court's right side. Stella practically flew through the air, intercepted her opponent, scoring a direct hit. 30/love. Stella delivered a cross-shot; Catalina failed to reach it before it went out of bounds. 40/love. Stella and Catalina battled the next serve. Stella's strength was more muscular than Catalina's. Years of weight lifting were paying off. Catalina's tank was full of gas, but she showed no activity; she looked slug-gish. Stella out-performed her, winning the point and the game. Stella's game had just warmed up. Stella was gaining ground fast; she won the next three games. Austin was fuming; *She's turned her back on nine. Catalina's head looks like a balloon, and when that happens to a tennis player, the only outcome is to wait for it to pop.*

Rhett and the company were consuming snacks while watching the game. "So tell us, Rhett, how's your little star going to get out of this one?"

Rhett stopped drinking from his straw and said, "All she has to do is win the next five games."

Catalina was sitting on the bench, talking to Austin and Grace. "We didn't come all this way to lose," said Austin. "You just lost three games."

"I can beat her without using nine," said Catalina.

"Ya! And how's that working out for you?" said Austin. Austin looked at Grace and thought, *You can coach her. I'm heading back to my chair.*

Austin returns to his seat while Grace tried to talk to Catalina. "I lost my tournament for the same reason you're losing this match," said Grace. "My weaknesses were the winner. Stella is too strong; that's your weakness. Your strength is nine squares. That's Stella's weakness. We have five games to win; we need to get started, follow my hand signs." Grace smiled. "She can't beat us both."

Catalina's come-back serve reached a top speed of 104 mph. Stella's generosity gave the ball back to Catalina. Cat returned the hit and quickly reacted, hitting square 4, setting nine in motion. Stella read the impact and headed for square 4; Cat ran for the net and intercepted the return, steering the attack towards square 3 for the win. 15/love. Austin turned towards Savanna and said, "And she wanted to do it the hard way."

But he knew the odds were still against her. Nine squares became the wrecking ball, tearing down years of training. Stella's face showed signs of defeat after Catalina continued her dominance over her now weaker opponent by dominating the match, winning six games to four, taking the first set.

In the announcer's booth, Rhett was smiling. "I think Vivian Green is in trouble."

"It's not over yet," said John.

Rhett questioned his friend. "Have you ever seen Vivian play like that?"

John said, "Yes, I have."

Rhett smiled. "Don't you have anything to do?"

John received Rhett's message loud and clear.

Grace's hands were full of hot dogs and popcorn and soda. She looked like a walking food court. Austin reached out for help grabbing the hotdogs. "A gourmet meal at its finest," said Grace.

With movement on the court, the second set was about to begin. Stella lost the coin toss again; most of us call it bad luck. Catalina's ego was more massive than life. Everything fell in place. Her challenger was crying on the inside. She was letting fifteen-year-old, unknown tennis players get the best of her. Every time Stella tried to score, Catalina intercepted using line shots and nine squares. Stella was no longer the number two player in the world. Catalina was in the finals. Flashing camera bulbs were everywhere; it was as glamorous as a Hollywood premiere. A fifteen-year-old star has emerged. Her fans surrounded her with pens and markers, trying to grab an autograph. "Do you have a pin?" asked Grace.

Austin responded, "Why do you need a pin?"

"We're going to have to pop her before the next match," laughed Grace.

Savanna loved humor, giving Grace a thumbs up as she laughed.

"Get comfortable; we're going to be a while," says Austin.

After celebrating with a late dinner, the ride to the hotel was full of laugher and joy. Catalina's eyes were wider than usual as she asked, "How much did I win tonight?"

Catalina watched Austin's face in the rearview mirror; her eyes were reading his lips as he said, "800,000 dollars." Catalina's body shivered with belief. Austin smiled at his lovely wife. Savanna knew what he was thinking. His dream was becoming a reality; it wasn't about the money; it was about the player.

CHAPTER 27

Lying in bed watching the sports channel, Austin was waiting for the coverage on the U.S. Open. "Finally," said Austin, turning up the sound. The headline news was all Catalina. They were labeling her as the next superstar in the future. While other stations were calling her lucky and giving her no chance against the number one ranked Vivian Green.

"Please don't listen to them," said Savanna.

Austins said, "We need to listen to them; they're right."

The weather was picture-perfect on this beautiful Saturday afternoon, with no wind. Birds were singing; sprinklers were watering; butterflies were searching for food.

Catalina's fan base was growing healthier by the minute. Empty seats would become full. In four hours or less, there would be a champion. All the commotion floating in the air was about the women's finals being more popular than the men's. The tournament has seen great young players before. But this young fifteen-year-old has never been in a match to this extreme in her life. Austin eyed his iPhone to check the time. He said, "I have little more than an hour and a half." Austin called out to Grace and Catalina, "Come over here, follow me." They were heading out of the stadium. "Come quickly!" said Austin.

"What are we doing in court three?" said Grace.

"Catalina versus nine squares," said Austin. "Grace and I will throw balls at you, hit the ball back to one of the nine squares, that I call it out."

"Do we have to do this an hour and a half before the match?" questioned Catalina.

"You almost lost that last match because you didn't use nine squares," said Austin. Catalina walked to the other side of the court. "Let's begin," yelled out Austin.

Standing by the fence post watching was Rhett Young, the announcer. He has never seen a training method quite like this before; no matter where Catalina was on the court, she hit it back to a number between 1 and 9. Perhaps these nine squares that Catalina spoke about last week and then hushed up. According to the numbers that sounded off, nine make-believe squares on each side of the court. Looking at the time, Rhett headed back to the announcer booth.

Heading back towards Arthur Stadium, Austin and the girls heard Rhett calling out on the loudspeakers; "Catalina, you're wanted in the women's finals."

Rhett says to John in the booth, "I can't believe I just said that." He laughed. In his double padded brown office chair with a view, Rhett was drawing a tennis court with a ruler and then adding nine squares on each side. He still didn't understand how it worked. Rhett's head turned toward the wall clock. Ten minutes before play, and no sign of Catalina and coach.

Austin faced Catalina and said, "Green is going to try to win this in two sets. We don't care that Greens number one. She has two arms and two legs just like you; nine squares will wear her down; it's your job to keep her running after it. Just focus on making nine squares work. No matter what the score is, you must keep applying nine squares. Do I make myself clear? You can win this match," said Austin.

Catalina nodded her head as to say yes.

"I gave you all the tools; your heart will determine your actions." Austin wiped away his tears; he smiled, then said, "Win." Grace, Catalina, and Austin smiled, then laughed. "Let's go; we're late to your final," said Austin.

CHAPTER 28

According to the cheers of the crowd, Catalina was the long-shot favorite. The group was chanting her name as she walked on to the court in her bright white outfit that said the champion. Catalina was waving to her fans. Vivian was talking in her mind: *When I get done with this girl, they will be calling out my name.*

Catalina ran past the referee, threw down her bag on the bench, and pulled out her blue racket with a bright white grip. Then headed toward the coin toss. "Heads it is," called out the judge. "Vivian serves first."

Arthur Ashe Stadium was full. Twenty-three thousand seats, the largest tennis venue in the U.S. Catalina was overwhelmed by the crowd. Austin yelled out, "Catalina! Pay attention!" Austin said to Grace, "That kid was floating somewhere," he laughs.

Savanna, witnessing her man fulfilling his dream was breathless. That's the man she married. If Catalina wins or loses, we can put nine squares to bed, and I know he can live with that.

There's only one word to describe Vivian Green: fast. Six foot three, and most of that was legs. She looked like a bodybuilder with a giant fly swatter in her hand. And if she won, this would be her fourth grand slam this year. Number 1 well deserved.

Silence filled the stadium as Vivian's yellow ball was thrown into the sky. All eyes were watching Catalina as she tried to defend herself from a ruthless force of power. Vivian's serve topped 106 mph. Catalina felt the wind from the ball, but nothing else. Vivian scoresd the first point 15/love. Catalina prepared herself for serve number two by taking a step backward to absorb the serve. She wasn't going to make the same mistake twice. Standing like a baseball player with two hands on the racket, Catalina was ready. Catalina returned the 104 mph serve with boldness and grit; the war had begun. Catalina was getting frustrated. Every time she tried to activate nine squares, she was rejected by Vivian. Vivian's backhand was as good as her forehand. She ripped the ball down the line for the point. 30/love. Vivian's next point, disguised as a curveball, broke early to avoid Catalina's swing blowing past her. 40/love. Catalina concentration was becoming extinct; it needed safeguarding, with a good shot of nine squares. Vivian's eyes glowed with determination. She knew if Catalina didn't score in the first game, Vivian would win her fourth grand slam. Catalina returned the ball; that looked like a rocket that just launched. Vivian's actions were dealing with one particular thing, hitting the ball over the net. Catalina was focusing on nine squares. She saw an opening in squares 1, 2, and 3. Catalina ran like a cheetah towards the net to block Vivian's return, plus setting up nine with 1, 2, and 3 squares. Catalina succeeded by catching the ball on the end of her racket, then dropping it down in front of the net on square 2. Cat won the point 40/15. Vivian yelled out, "A lucky shot!"

Catalina turned around and said, "I'll take all the luck I can get," as she grinned widely.

At that moment in time, Catalina's faces lit up like LEDs that glowed confidence. The crowd started chanting, "Catalina!"

The madness began to dig a deep hole; It produces adrenaline; it increases blood flow to the muscles and the heart by binding to alpha and beta receptors. The radar machine clocked the ball 106 mph from Vivian's serve. Catalina's swing was slower than the ball. Vivian won the first game. Austin called for a 3-minute break.

Austin and Grace walked towards Catalina. Inside their huddle, Austin said, "You need to wear her out, or you'll lose. If we wear her down, we can catch her using nine squares; we have plenty of time."

"She's running down the ball and cuts off nine," said Catalina.

"We need to slow her down," said Austin as he thought of a strategy. "Every shot from you has to be a nine-shot. It would cause Vivian to run in circles; by the end of three games, she'll be tired, we hope," said Austin. "Remember the three components of nine squares. Easy, difficult, and hard. Your hard shots fall in squares 1 and 3. Difficult uses square 4 or 6. Easy, 7, and 9. It depends on where Vivian is standing. It would help if you took a risk; you have three choices. You're doing great; this is how it's supposed to work." Austin smiled, then said, "It's your time. Go make history. Now go back out there and win."

The second game started similarly. Vivian's strength and talent continue to dominate the open. Vivian was running all over the court, engulfed by Catalina's plan to wear her down. Vivian continued to dominate by winning three consecutive games; the number one player in the world was still in control. Catalina could see Vivian starting to fade a little. Catalina needed two wins from her serve and two wins from nine squares. Catalina eyes her trainer and her best friend. She dug deep down and grabbed her inner soul, throwing the ball free from any flaw. Her serve stepped on the gas, hitting the radar gun, 106 mph. Vivian, for the first time, barely returned the ball. Catalina's computer (her mind) pinpointed a nine-square kill shot. Catalina was going after Vivian's backhand with a line shot on the backside of square

9; Vivian took a fall from overrunning as it hit its target. Time out, while the paramedics put a band-aid on her bleeding knee. 15/love.

Rhett was studying Catalina's nine squares system when all of a sudden, the light turned on before his eyes. You must drive the other player to one of the nine squares to keep her from reaching a second shot. "Genius, but simple," said Rhett. "She's trying to wear her out with nine squares, then use the same system to win. The last point with Vivian was proof that nine worked."

Austin said to Grace, "That little knee bruise will be on her mind the whole game; that's just what we needed, a distraction."

"Let the play continue," said a large voice springing from the loud speakers. Catalina had to stay focused. Win or lose, she had to follow the game plan. Catalina laid down rubber-like a drag racer with a smoking serve, hitting the outer line for the point. 30/love. Catalina's third serve forced a rally. Catalina was keeping up with her more prominent opponent. Nine squares kept Vivian running to all four corners of the court. Catalina slammed the yellow ball on square 4; only Vivian's long arms reached the shot. Catalina quickly jumped on the ball, then aimed her racket towards square 9, hitting the win line. The crowd exploded with excitement. 40/Love. For the first time, Vivian was showing signs of frustration. Catalina looked at Grace. She's shaking her head up and down; the head jester says: take Vivian down. Catalina rifled a hard shot, jamming Vivian's return and winning the point. Catalina won her first game.

Vivian returned the favor with a 105 mph serve blowing past Catalina like a tornado. Vivian grinned at Catalina. 15/love. Catalina had the appearance of being the runner-up.

It wasn't about the dog in the fight; it was about the fight in the dog. Vivian's backhand was a weapon. It seemed like her shots were laser-guided from a destroyer hundreds of miles away. Catalina returned Vivian's second serve aiming at square 6, then ran to the net's front right side, hoping for a break. Vivian saw Catalina planting her feet in front of the net. Catalina handed over her racket to her left hand to reach the ball, a move that she had never tried before. Austin had to see it to believe it; she was playing left-handed. A full swing with her left hand drove the ball down the left sideline for the point. A textbook shot that would be called the Catalina. 15/15. The hotdog-eating crowd was on the edge of their seats all over the stadium, wondering if tomorrow's headline would be history in the making. Vivian kept forcing the game on Catalina with direct shots, cramming Catalina and forcing her to make errors. A tied game now became Vivian's advantage 40/15. Her next serve started a long rally. Everyone was waiting for some response from Catalina, who was drowning in a puddle of sweat. Catalina hit a longer than needed shot past the boundaries. Vivian won the fifth game, giving her a four games to one lead. Catalina continued the balls' battle, trying to get the upper hand by setting up nine squares from every angle. Vivian's persistence and speed were winning out over her younger opponent. Vivian won the first set, six games to one.

As the two players were drinking water before changing sides, Grace had a small opportunity to grab Catalina's ear with encouragement. Austin and Savanna noticed Grace's actions. Austin stood up, only to be pulled down by the hand of Savanna. "Let them talk," said Savanna.

No sound came from Austin, only thoughts. Austin sat back down. Grace smiled in front of Catalina and then told a story about a young girl who played tennis in the snow. Grace asked, "Why did you do that?"

Catalina answered, "Because I wanted to be a champion."

"Do you still want to be a champion?" said Grace.

"Yes," said Catalina.

Grace replied, "You better get started."

Catalina grinned big with teardrops falling from her eyes.

Catalina stood up and walked across the court. Catalina had a renewed look on her face. That's the look Austin had seen all year long. Catalina would serve first, starting the second set. She needed to win, or it was going home for Catalina.

Catalina served in a straight line. Vivian strong armed the perfect shot back over the net. Catalina's consequence would determine her outcome. Catalina laid down the groundwork for nine squares, sending the ball flying through the air without a plane. The ball hit square 6. Vivian's pace was beginning to work against her. The line shots were winning; Vivian was a step behind. Catalina won the point 15/15. Catalina continued to dominate the first game.

Nine squares and Catalina were climbing the scoreboard. Catalina's serve bounced off the rigid surface. Vivian tried the strongman's move with a low short guttural sound. Returning the ball would have worked if the net didn't get in the way. Catalina won the first game. Catalina lost the next two games by small margins; it didn't seem like nine squares were slowing Vivian down. Vivian was getting ready to serve game four. If she won four more games, Vivian would win all four Grand Slams in one year.

As Vivian continued to serve, Catalina continued setting up nine squares. Catalina's shots were becoming more accurate and taking more of a chance. She beat Vivian in game four to tie the score, two, two. Vivian and Catalina battled with hard hits shots flying back and forth all over the court. Catalina kept up the pressure. Hearing her coach's voice from the past, she remembered him saying, *Nine will wear her out, don't let up.* Catalina hit two net shots in a row and lost the game. Three games to two.

Everyone knew Catalina was just three games away from being eliminated. Vivian's mind and body were tired of this young tennis player. After stuffing one tennis ball down her pocket as a spare, Vivian was ready to go home. But, she had a small problem; she had a thorn in her side, a young fifteen-year-old named Catalina.

Catalina took her stance. She must defend herself regardless of what it looks like on the outside. Catalina's mind moved her lips, saying, "She is just a tennis player; I can beat her."

Vivian unleashed a straightforward spinning ball in Catalina's direction. Catalina rushed the net and leaped in front of the ball, rolling it off her racket and dripping on square 2. Catalina's point, love/15. After hitting Vivian's serve, Cat jumped forward again, racing toward the net, trying to second-guess the incoming ball. It was a backhanded shot on the left side of the court. Cat switched hands with the racket and reached until it hurts, stopping the speeding ball in its tracks, then allowing Catalina to place the yellow ball in square 1 for the win. Love/30. Austin knew Catalina's plan. She was playing the hard squares. The only trouble is running to the net; every serve will wear you out. It was just a matter of time before Vivian started aiming over her head. For a third time, Catalina rushed to the court's center following an excellent serve from Vivian. Catalina's racket blocked the ball like a worker holding up a sign along the highway. The ball dropped on square 2. Vivian was two steps away from losing. Catalina scored love/40. Vivian was on edge; she can't remember the last time she lost a game without scoring. An 101 mph serve visited Catalina, who quickly told the ball to go home. She knew the return function was on; the tennis net had become her friend. Catalina aggressively ran towards her friend. Vivian's muscles pulled back, causing a chain reaction as Vivian watched her ball fall into the net. Catalina won the game; they were tied three games apiece. Catalina began to set up nine squares after one return, knowing it would be risky. She was running out of time. Catalina's thoughts were her potent weapon. Both are powerful but don't forget; there would be no weapon without our thoughts. Catalina's serve reached 103 mph. Vivian jumped ahead, hit the shot, ran towards the net, and blocked Catalina's ball. Love/15. Vivian returned the second ball fired off by Catalina. It hit the outside line for the win. Love/30. Moments after serving, Catalina attacked the net. Vivian popped a high fly over Catalina's head. Catalina turned around, and then headed for the ball with one arm stretched out, and popped the ball over Vivian's head, falling on Vivian's 9 square for the win. 15/30. Vivian gave the next ball to the net. 30/30. Catalina waited for the fifth serve eagerly. Catalina walloped the artificial round ball with felt towards square 9. Vivian reached the ball; the only problem was she was still running the wrong way after hitting. Catalina eyed square 4, then hit a beautiful sideways shot before the line, then bounces out of bounds. 40/30. Catalina's face looked down; she summoned her Lord Jesus Christ, her strength, her peace of mind. He gives dreams to everyone; this dream was Catalina's. God gives you the plan. That means it's already happened in his eyes.

Catalina's serve becoming more assertive. Vivian's ball stopped at the net. Catalina won the point and the game—four games to three. Catalina took the lead for the first time. Bracing for attacks, Catalina cemented her feet into the court. Vivian's ball raised into the air like a weather balloon. Vivian slapped a screamer over the net, heading directly in front of Catalina. Cat hit a steady line drive waiting for an opening for nine. Realizing nine squares was in trouble, Cat ran for the net and cut off Vivian's return. Catalina scored, Love/15. Vivian's energy level read two bars; her serves were slowing down;

her steps were closer together. Vivian's second attempt to take back this game was invalid. Catalina was taking charge by continuing to wear Vivian down. Vivian was blowing points. Catalina continued to bring down the giant, forcing her to fall off the bean stalk. Catalina won the next two points. Love/40. Serving with desperation was new for Vivian. She hadn't been sunk on a game since she was an amateur. Vivian catapulted her serve with extreme speed, hitting the outside line. 15/40. Catalina gained her composure by hitting her next shot toward square 7, which gave her time to rush the net and pounded the ball into square 1; Vivian gave up seconds earlier. Catalina took the lead five games to three. The crowd was on pins and needles. Catalina was one game away from tying the world's most significant player. Catalina's mind was trained for this very moment in time. Not by chance or an accident, but by the Grace of God.

Catalina eyed Austin, Austin eyed Grace. Heads nodded up and down. Catalina knew the plan well. Eight months, twelve to fifteen-hour days. Her first name might as well be Nine. And by the way, no one told her she was fifteen and inexperienced. Catalina's gas tank was on reserve. The question remained how long before empty.

Vivian hits Catalina's serve back over the net. Catalina rushed the net and missed Vivian's shot. Vivian's point, love/15. Catalina delivered a straight horizontal shot in front of Vivian; again, Catalina rushed the net, this time, she won. 15/15. Catalina ran for the net and scored with a sideways shot ending in front of the net. 30/15. Catalina hoped racing to the net would be the demise of Vivian, who was running all over the court on the command of a fifteen-year-old. The battle raged as if two tanks were facing each other on the battlefield. Catalina threw up a rubber ball covered with flannel-stitched skin and sent it flying through the air with complete accuracy. Vivian hammered it back to the other side of the court. Catalina erasered the recorded material from her mind on rushing the net. Catalina began to make her move and set up nine. Cat dropped a soft hit on square 3, forcing Vivian to come near the net. Vivian could see the writing on the wall.

She had no choice; she had to run for the ball, knowing Cat was going to strike deep. Catalina's sets up of nine was perfect; square 7 was wide open. She scored, 40/15. Catalina served as if it was her first serve. Full of energy and excitement. The crowd was amazed; the flannel ball landed as a category one hurricane, packing speeds of 106 mph. Vivian's return heads out of bounds. Thousands cheered as Catalina won the point and the set.

The excitement was shining from the announcer's booth. Rhett and his colleagues were wowing. Vivian just lost the second set. Rhett turned his chair and said to John, "Now we have a match."

Down on the sidelines, Austin, Grace, and, of course, Catalina were in a tennis huddle, a close-knit group with no outsiders. Austin looked deep into Catalina's eyes. With tears deriving from the circumstances, Austin said, "Your mind and your body must become one. You just beat the number one player in the world. You just have to beat her one more time."

"Snowball," said Grace. Catalina didn't understand. "When you hit the ball in the snow nine months ago, you had to visualize the outcome. Snowball and nine are a winning combination," smiled Grace.

Austin was wordless, then said, "Win or lose, I'm proud of you. And by the way, if you beat her, it's worth three million dollars."

Catalina's face glowed eagerness. Austin needed the push her exhilaration button. It was the only card that he has left.

Catalina positioned herself to defeat her opponent. Vivian has never been in this predicament before. The spectators were chanting "Catalina!" Vivian's aggressiveness was no secret. A complete powerhouse when she turned it on. Vivian started the game with a deep line shot. Catalina was far enough back to absorb the impact. Catalina's return leveled out on its return flight home. Catalina quickly moved into nine position. Vivian hit from square 8. Catalina hit it to square 7; then, she ran for the net, blocking it like a dam. She hit Vivian's return with a sideways shot on square 6 for the win. Catalina took the first point, love/15. Vivian dug deep; her next serve clocked at 106 mph. It aced Catalina for the win, 15/15. Vivian gestured to the crowd with her right hand. She was telling them she was here to win. Catalina prepared herself for the battle that lies in front of her. She returned Vivian's serve; Vivian aimed the ball at the sideline; she hit her target, Vivian scored. 30/15.Vivian again out-powered Catalina with a strong serve, blowing past Catalina for the win. 40/15. After Vivian's next serve, Vivian ran to the net and jumped in front of the ball, blocked it; it fell on Catalina's side of the net for the point. Vivian had won the first game with ease. She was five games away from her fourth Grand Slam title.

Catalina's mind reflects on what Grace had said about the snow in the park. Visualize the win before it happens. Catalina's first serve reached the other side safely, only to be outgunned by Vivian's strength. As Catalina traveled to the court's front, Vivian nailed a perfect shot over Catalina for the win. Love/15. Vivian borrowed Cat's idea of running up to the net for the block. Catalina's nerves played against her as she choked by hitting the ball into the net, love/30. Vivian continued her attack, using the net as self-defense. Catalina seemed helpless; setting up nine was almost impossible with Vivian attacking the net. She had to drive Vivian away from the net if she had any hope of winning. Vivian took the next two points. She won the second game.

Austin looked at Savanna as his thoughts passed through his lips. He said, "She is unable to defend herself from the net. Nine squares have an imperfection."

Austin rose from his seat. "Where are you going?" asked Savanna.

"She needs help," said Austin. "I got her in this mess. I have to get her out."

Austin signaled Grace to follow him out of the stadium. Catalina saw the two of them walking off as she got ready for game three. Austin verbalized by speaking out loud. "We have to get Vivian off the net, any suggestions?"

Grace thought for a second. "She needs to pop it over her head, which would force her backward and give Cat time to set up nine squares," says Grace.

Austin's left eyebrow lifted. "If she gets excited under pressure and pops it's too far, she'll lose the game," said Austin.

Grace smiled. "She's already losing."

Grace and Austin headed back to the stadium, knowing he couldn't talk to Catalina until the next game was over. Austin glanced at the scoreboard. Catalina was down 30/40 in game three. Catalina's next serve forced Vivian to play deep. After two rallies, Catalina was able to set nine squares in motion with a sideways line shot that fell into the hands of a ball boy. The score was now deuce, 40/40. Realizing the net was her best option, Vivian again attacked the net and stopped Catalina in her tracks, winning the next two serves. Vivian won the third game. The score was three games to zero.

Austin walked along the outer court, heading for Catalina as she gulped down a bottle of water. Catalina had a look of uncertainty. Austin sat beside her and said, "You need to force her back with a popup over her head when she runs for the net, but not too far. That will give you one chance to set nine squares in motion. If you hit it out of bounds, she's the winner. She's yours for the taking."

Vivian served with ferocity. Catalina returned a substantial hit; Catalina noticed Vivian was standing still after Vivian sent the ball in her direction. Cat aimed for the tip of square 6 and hit her target. Catalina took the lead 15/love. After Vivian's second return, she ran for the net. Grace and Austin were holding their breath. Catalina has never done a popup on purpose in a tournament in her life. It was as graceful as a bird in flight. Flying over Vivian's head and out of reach of her racket, and falling on square 7 for the win. Austin tightened his fingers; he had the feeling of winning. Catalina continued her comeback one point at a time. Switching from right-handed to southpaw was throwing Vivian off, and advancing to the net and setting nine squares in motion was working. She was the new popup queen, setting up nine, winning with nine. Catalina advanced three straight games in a row. Vivian took the next game pulling into the lead four games to three. Catalina was getting tired; her knees were hurting, her arms were sore. She was hanging on to a dream that had no retreat. God gave her the plan before she was born.

Vivian was now two games away from being crowned the champion. A lengthy and challenging conflict was about to unfold. Catalina started gaining again by winning the next game by two points. They tied four games apiece.

Rhett looked over at John and said, "She's going to win. I'll bet my paycheck on it! Did you see all the popups she was doing right over Vivian's head? Was she nailing them? Plus, I've never seen a player switch hands playing tennis." Rhett had to stop talking; the game was about to start; he was the voice.

Vivian felt she had faced more formidable opponents than Catalina; Catalina's only difference was challenging to believe. Vivian started the next game with a clear shot in front of Catalina. Catalina quickly returned the ball with a decisive grunt; she aimed for square 4 to draw Vivian to the outside. Vivian showed her greatness by returning the shot in four steps. Catalina countered with a clean shot toward the back of the court; it landed on square nine for the point, Catalina leads, love/15. The crowd erupted, clapping and chanting Catalina's name. Rhett had to quiet the public from the loudspeakers. Vivian's serve reached its potential as Catalina quickly and forcefully hit the top of the net and dribbled the ball on Vivian's side. A lucky point for Catalina. Love/30. After Vivian's next serve, she leaped for her side of the net to achieve her goal, which was to stop Catalina. Catalina pretended to lob it over Vivian's head, Vivian retreated, and Catalina cuts the ball sideways just past the net on Vivian's side, for the point, love /40. The crowd exploded with excitement. Catalina lost the next two serves as Vivian power-housed the young athlete. 30/40. Vivian's sixth serve hit the net. Catalina knew the second serve would land softer. She heard Austin in the background; his words are generating the command: *Nine.* The two opponents played the game back and forth. Their muscles were on rations. Catalina visualized nine leading the way and finally saw an opening on square 6. Vivian counter-attacked, knowing Cats' plan. But there was nothing she could do once the ball was in motion. Catalina gunned the ball toward square 6 while keeping its distance from Vivian. Catalina won the game. She led five games to four.

The crowd jumps out of their seat, chanting Catalina's name. The whole stadium was high on excitement, the talk of the town.

Austin yelled out to Catalina, "Snow!" She knew what he was saying, "Visualize nine squares."

Savanna's emotions were crying. The crowd was roaring with excitement. It was the match of the decade. Catalina would serve for the win. The crowd quickly silenced in anticipation. She had to stay focused. Catalina bounced the ball twice, then looked up. Her opponent and herself locked eyes. Catalina's next serve inched above the white part of the net and streamed towards Vivian. Vivian's return traveled to the deep lift side of the court. Catalina slammed the ball back and began setting up nine squares by hitting the ball toward Vivian's backhand on the left side. Catalina took a chance on square 4, then ran for the net to trap Vivian's shot, then forced the ball towards square 6 for the win. The crowd erupted like a volcano. Catalina won the first point, 15/love. Walking to the back of the court, Catalina nodded at Austin. His heart jumped a beat. Austin grabbed Savanna's hand and squeezed it. Well, he was keeping his eyes on the game. Catalina's next serve met Vivian's wallop, with a line shot that bounced off Cats racket and headed out of bounds. The game was tied 15/15. Catalina gained her composure, served, and received the same result as Vivian ran for the net and scooted the yellow ball with her backhand; the ball landed in bounds and then darted out of bounds for the point. Vivian led 15/30. Austin bowed his head then spoke to Savanna. For the first time in his life, he couldn't help. Tears rolled down Austin's eyes. Catalina rubbed her hand over the top of her head and grabbed her ponytail; her inner fight was harnessing. She was three points from winning the U.S. Open. It was now or never as her determination expanded. Catalina visualized her next serve. If she was to win, her first return had to set up nine squares.

Following Catalina's serve, Vivian tried to manhandle Catalina with a firm shot to the court's left side, trying to deflate Cat's energy. Catalina was running sporadically all over the court. Catalina backhanded a blind shot that landed on square 6. Vivian responded with a straight line shot with an almost impossible forward shot from Catalina that hit its mark, landing on square 4; it would take a bullet to outrun the yellow ball. Catalina won, 30/30. The crowd was cheering so loud that people could hear cheering a mile away.

Cat remembered what the coach had said: the most challenging squares to hit were 1, 2, and 3; this may sound crazy, but Catalina needed Vivian to attack the net to set up nine squares.

Catalina began with a hard hit, trying to knock Vivian off her pedestal. Vivian swatted the ball in Cats' direction. Catalina took a half swing, hoping to avoid the net in front of her and forcing Vivian off her pedestal. Vivian escalated to the front of the court. Catalina had no choice; she needed a popup to reach a limited space behind Vivian. Catalina needed a perfect shot, or Vivian's long arms would foil the plot. Catalina popped the ball over Vivian's head; time slowed down to almost a stopping point. Every eye in the stadium was watching the ball—Vivian raced backward to save the game. Vivian hit a high blind shot seven feet over her head, landing on Cats' side of the court. Catalina rushed the ball. She had a tiny margin on delivering the ball on square 1. Catalina visualized the win in her mind, and without looking, used two hands on a racket that resembled a baseball swing. She hit the outer line by a quarter of an inch to win the point. 40/30.

Grace jumped out of her seat with the rest of the crowd. Austin yelled out at the top of her lungs, "Nine!" The crowd ingested Austin's words. Seconds later, the crowd cheered and chanted Catalina's name. As silence entered the air, Rhett and John were standing at the helm in a suspended state. Austin and Savanna felt like they were standing on the edge of a cliff, hoping they wouldn't fall.

Catalina looked over at Grace, Grace gave her a thumbs up. Catalina stared at Austin. He touched his index finger on his temple, then shows nine fingers, then clenched his fist. Catalina nodded her head. Austin sat down, holding Savanna's hand. Catalina shut her eyes to visualize the win. Opening up her eyes, she could see Vivian standing in front of her. All the negative thoughts packed up and went home. Catalina smiled; Austin knew that was pure confidence. She bounced the ball three times, which would become her trademark. Vivian was expecting a big serve. Catalina would fool her and Austin by unleashing a slower serve to set up nine squares; if she were going to win, she needed to do it with nine squares. Her next shot was for the coach. Vivian returned the ball with a deep shot that lands on the backline. Catalina pounded the yellow ball over the net. Vivian stayed in the fight and hit a hard shot trying to take down Catalina. Catalina saw a clear victory with an opening on square 9; she gripped her racket with two hands and delivered a rock-hard hit that landed on square 9. Vivian moved like the wind toward the ball. In the meantime, Catalina's eyed square 4. Vivian aimed the ball toward Catalina's backhand, trying to unseat her opponent. Catalina squinted as her backhand followed her inner vision; she visualized the outer line on square 4. Austin was biting his lip; Grace stood up; Savanna squeezed her husband's hand. The crowd looked like a photo. Rhett was speechless for the first time in his life. Catalina swung with her eyes closed; the yellow ball bounces half way on the line, too close to call. Was it out, or was it in? Catalina's dream was on hold. Vivian called for a review. Austin jumped out of his seat and ran toward the judge to argue the call. Grace stands next to Savanna, waiting on the outcome. After reviewing Catalina's return, the judge said, "It's good."

Austin hugs Catalina; both were crying. Grace and Savanna jump out of their seats and ran in between them; they were crying. The crowd rushed on the court, picking Catalina up and carrying her around the court. Austin, Savanna, and Grace hold each other with a shower of tears flowing out of their eyes. Rhett wiped his eyes with his finger after hugging John. "Wow," said Rhett. "I've never seen anything like that in my life."

Catalina received her trophy and a check for three million dollars. She could not stop shaking as she held up her award. It was a photo moment that would last a lifetime. The President handed her the mic to give a speech. With tears running down her face, she said thank you to her fans. Then said, "Nine months ago, a stranger entered my life with a crazy idea that I could win the U.S. Open. All because I was playing tennis in the snow. As crazy as that sounds, that's true. That man is my coach, coach Austin. Thank you. And I wouldn't be here without my best friend and tennis coach, Grace, thank you."

The crowd applauded their new champion.

Two weeks later, Austin was sitting on his porch drinking coffee when he heard a bicycle horn beeping. Grace was riding her bike, and Catalina was behind riding her skateboard. The girls stopped on the sidewalk in front of Austin's house. Austin was surprised by the visit. He was glad to see the girls. The three of them laughed and talked about the tournament, when all of a sudden, Catalina said, "Can I ask you a question?"

"Shoot away," said Austin.

"Why did you believe in me?" asked Catalina.

"I've never seen anyone play tennis in the snow. Either you were mentally deranged, or you had the courage and resolve to make nine squares work, and that's why I believed in you." Catalina's eyes filled with tears. "And by the way, Grace, I expect you to play Catalina in the finals next year." Grace smiled. "Is your mom enjoying her new home?"

Catalina wiped her eyes. "She loves her new home; she is now retired," said Catalina.

Austin hugged Catalina; his life had love, and joy, and closure from a 35-year-old theory called Nine Squares. "Monday morning, at ten o'clock in the park. We have a lot of work to do," said Austin. "But in the meantime, Savanna just pulled an apple pie out of to oven. Would you like a piece?"

Both girls lit up like a Christmas tree. "Yes!" said the girls.

As all three of them walked into the house for some pie, Austin said, "You need a car. I can't have the U.S. tennis champion riding a skateboard; when do you turn sixteen?"

"Next month," said Catalina. "I have a car on order."

"You don't say," said Austin. "What kind?"

Catalina and Grace smiled at each other. Catalina said, "A red Porsche."

Austin laughed. "You've earned it."

THE END